YOURS AND MINE

IN DOG TOWN

SANDY RIDEOUT

ELLEN RIGGS

FREE PREQUEL

A Rescue Dog and an Unexpected Date with Destiny

Meet Isla McInnis, a reporter who flies across the country to Dorset Hills on a hunch that a sweet little rescue dog named Rio will change her life forever. A quirky band of rescue rebels shows her the true reason she was called to this quaint town in the first place. Join Sandy Rideout's author newsletter at **Sandyrideout.com** to get the FREE PREQUEL to the Dog Town cozy-romance series at sandyrideout.com.

Yours and Mine in Dog Town

ISBN 978-1-989303-01-6 eBook
ISBN 978-1-989303-02-3 Book
ASIN B07HLFK9KS Kindle
ASIN 1989303021 Paperback

Publisher: Sandy Rideout
www.sandyrideout.com
Cover designer: Lou Harper
Editor: Serena Clarke
2103120100

WELCOME TO DOG TOWN!

Dear Reader,

I used to be a diehard cat lady. Then I got my first dog ever and I was a goner! A journalist by training, I interviewed every expert I could find: trainers, breeders, groomers, walkers and more. The journey ultimately brought me here, to Dog Town.

Dorset Hills, better known as *Dog Town*, is famous for being the most dog-friendly place in the world. People come from near and far to enjoy its beautiful landscape and unique charms. Naturally, when so many dogs and dog-lovers unite in one town, mischief and mayhem ensue.

In the Dog Town cozy-romance series, you can expect the humor, the quirky, loveable characters and the edge-of-your-seat suspense that are part of any cozy mystery, but there's a little more romance and a lot less murder. In fact, *no one dies*! I can guarantee you'll laugh out loud and enjoy hair-raising adventures, heartwarming holidays and happily-ever-afters for both humans and pets.

You can read the books in any order, but it's more fun to work your way through the seasons in Dog Town:

- *Ready or Not in Dog Town* (The Beginning)
- *Bitter and Sweet in Dog Town* (Labor Day)
- *A Match Made in Dog Town* (Thanksgiving)

- *Lost and Found in Dog Town* (Christmas)
- *Calm and Bright in Dog Town* (Christmas)
- *Tried and True in Dog Town* (New Year's)
- *Yours and Mine in Dog Town* (Valentine's Day)
- *Nine Lives in Dog Town* (Easter)
- *Great and Small in Dog Town* (Memorial Day)
- *Bold and Blue in Dog Town* (Independence Day)
- *Better or Worse in Dog Town* (Labor Day)

If you fancy more murder with your mystery, be sure to join my newsletter at **Sandyrideout.com** to get the FREE PREQUEL to the Bought-the-Farm Cozy Mystery series. My newsletter is filled with funny stories and photos of my adorable dogs. Don't miss out!

Take care,
Sandy (and Ellen)

CHAPTER ONE

Few towns were prettier at Christmastime than Dorset Hills. Council turned the downtown core into something straight out of a fairy tale, with a massive tree in Bellington Square outside City Hall and enough lights sparkling on the quaint old buildings to imperil the electrical grid. It was a lot, yet somehow never too much. Dorset Hills always walked that fine line with skill and considerable style. That was how the town had grown into a small city that was now known as the best place in all of North America for dogs and dog-lovers.

For the entire month of December, Main Street bustled with shoppers in puffy down coats. Their colorful hats, mittens and scarves often matched their dogs' winter wear and accessories. It wasn't meant to be ironic. In Dog Town, looking like your canine companion was something to be celebrated.

Each shop had a festive window display that competed to grab the most eyes. Small Wonders Boutique typically led the pack with its replica of the entire town in miniature. Children pressed their noses to the glass, arguing over which tiny, hand-painted dog was the cutest. The popular vote went to a pair of wire-haired dachshunds, and then something truly wondrous happened: they multiplied. After the litter of miniscule wiener dog puppies arrived in the window, sales at the boutique skyrocketed.

A mere 10 blocks away, the charm started to fizzle out. In "East Bellington," decorations were less stylish and more sporadic. By night, local pranksters often dressed up or otherwise defaced an eight-foot bronze statue of a Mexican hairless dog that stood too close to a tavern for its own good. Where they found a bonnet and nightshirt that size was anyone's guess. The police deployed foot patrols to protect the dog from vandalism, but people found a way. There was a small faction of Dog Towners who couldn't simply enjoy a good thing.

Sasha Wildwood wasn't one of them. Ten months after her move to Dorset Hills, her love for the quirky community continued to grow by leaps and bounds. On December 24th, she stood inside the Pewter Poodle Grooming Salon wishing she'd pushed the owner harder to let her decorate. She'd offered to bring in a small tree and her own trimmings, but Mildred Trowbridge wouldn't hear of it. An indoor tree was too great a temptation for the dogs that filed in shabby and left pristine. Sasha saw the sense in that, but it was her first Dog Town Christmas and she wanted to get the most out of the season.

"One day I'll work on Main Street," she told the fluffy goldendoodle she'd just finished grooming. "You can come with me, Collette."

The dog looked like something off a magazine cover. Since finishing her grooming certification a few weeks earlier, Sasha had ticked off the classic precision clips for poodles, wheaten terriers, schnauzers and the like, but this was her first opportunity to be really creative. It had turned out so well that she felt better about her decision to change careers from hairstylist to groomer. Like many newcomers, she'd retrained to be marketable in the booming canine economy. She didn't miss the constant chitchat of human clients, but then again, humans never nipped.

A small movement made her jump. Mildred had emerged from her grooming room on stealthy feet. There was a horrified expression on her normally stony face.

"What is *that*?" Millie asked, staring down at Collette.

"A goldendoodle." Sasha wondered if it was a trick question. The gaunt, grey-haired woman wasn't known for her humor.

"No, *this* is a goldendoodle." Millie gestured to her own furry charge, a large hybrid named Maxwell. He looked tiny now, because Millie had sheared him down to the bone, except for a few strategically placed puffs. His muzzle was bare, his toes visible and his tail as naked as a rat's.

"I see you've gone with a standard poodle cut," Sasha said. "I did the teddy bear."

Collette did look huggable, with her clouds of golden fur ending in a gorgeous sweeping fan of tail.

"The what?"

"Teddy bear. I thought most doodle owners preferred it." She stared down at Maxwell. "They said so in grooming school."

"You've barely trimmed that dog at all." It sounded as if Millie was strangling what she really wanted to say.

Sasha hated confrontation, but the client came first. "This is what the owner asked for."

"Sasha. I know you're still new in town but we don't do those newfangled styles here. People like a classic look. I've never heard of a teddy bear cut. Did you make that up?"

"Actually, I call it my 'Muppet Aesthetic.' People see it and automatically go, 'awww.'"

"Muppet *what*?" Millie shook her head. "Never mind. Give me the dog and I'll fix that cut immediately. We can't have upset clients, especially on Christmas Eve."

Sasha moved her hand away as Millie tried to take the leash. "The owner showed me photos and I've done what she wanted."

"What they *think* they want and what they really want are two different things. She'd be back by Boxing Day demanding that dog be shaved down. Give her to me now."

Backing away, Sasha clutched the leash. "Please. Let the owner see her, first. If she's unhappy, I'll shave Collette right away. But you can't glue fur back on once it's gone."

"I simply can't have it. The dog looks like the cowardly lion from the Wizard of Oz."

Sasha looked down and laughed. "She does, a bit. That's perfect."

"This is no laughing matter. You give me that dog right now, young lady."

Pulling Collette along, Sasha moved into the corner. At 33, she was hardly a young lady, but she knew she came off that way. It was a blessing and a curse. "Millie, I quizzed the owner at length and she won't be happy if she finds Collette's been poodled."

Color flooded Mildred's sallow face. "Poodle isn't a verb. Not in my salon. I gave this dog a classic cut, which takes meticulous care. Meanwhile it looks like you hacked away with a blunt ax. The poor dog will be a laughing stock."

Maxwell was the one squirming. A close shave usually left a dog itchy and twitchy. His build was much heavier than a standard poodle's and Sasha thought he looked dreadful. And unhuggable. In her experience, owners of doodles tended to be huggers. They craved living teddy bears and it was her mission to deliver.

"You're sending Max out with no defense against a Dorset Hills winter," Sasha said.

"That's what jackets are for. There are entire shops devoted to selling them."

"Most dogs don't need jackets. That's what fur is for."

Millie dropped Maxwell's leash and took a lunge at Sasha. She was surprisingly agile for a woman well north of 60. Every morning she jogged with her own dog, a grey poodle. A well-kept poodle was a groomer's best advertisement, she'd told Sasha in their job interview. Sasha had nodded and smiled, and then smiled and nodded. Millie hadn't asked about Sasha's own dog. If she'd known Petunia was a Welsh springer spaniel—a dog that barely needed grooming at all—she probably wouldn't have hired her. In fact, she'd made it clear she only hired Sasha because she was desperate. With non-shedding dogs on the rise in Dorset Hills the demand for grooming services exceeded supply, especially around the holidays. Sasha had been desperate herself to get practice hours to complete her certification.

Millie took another lunge and this time her front teeth jutted like fangs. "You give me that dog right now."

Dodging quickly, Sasha ran around the counter with Collette frolicking alongside. "I will not. I'm putting the client first, just like you told me on my first day."

This time, Millie did a long jump from a standing position. If the door hadn't opened at that exact moment, Sasha likely would have lost the battle.

"How nice, you're all playing with Collette," the owner said, smiling as she brushed snow from her coat. "And she looks absolutely gorgeous, Sasha. This is exactly what I wanted... only better. It's like you read my mind."

"I'm so glad you like it," Sasha said. "Collette was a perfect darling."

The bell over the door rang again and a teenage girl came in with two friends. Suddenly the small shop was very crowded.

"Oh my gosh, Max looks amazing," the girl said, although she was staring down at Collette. "Oh, wait. That's not Max. Where is he? Oh no!" She fell on her knees beside her dog. "What happened? Was there an accident?"

Since Mildred was speechless, Sasha answered for her. "Millie gave Maxwell the classic poodle cut."

"But my mom asked for a trim! He looks awful. I didn't even recognize him."

Maxwell flinched as if he'd done something wrong, and Sasha came over to soothe him. "It's okay, Max. It's okay."

"It's not okay," the teen said. "You can see his skin."

"You can see his vital organs," one of her friends said, before the other one shushed her.

"It will grow back." Sasha had used that line a hundred times when human clients regretted their decision to 'cut it all off.' "You'll be surprised at how quickly."

The teen turned again to Collette. "*That's* what we wanted. She's like a teddy bear."

"When you come back we can do the same to Max," Sasha said. "Just give it time."

"How much time?" the teen asked.

"A few months." Sasha added under her breath, "Maybe six."

The girl glared at Mildred. "This is the worst Christmas ever. Thanks to you."

Millie edged behind the counter, looking stricken. She

let Sasha move in front of her and cash the two clients out. Sasha made small talk with Collette's owner and then saw her to the door. The woman hugged her and wished her a happy holiday.

When the door closed behind everyone, Sasha turned. "I'm so sorry, Mildred."

"You should be. I've never had a client behave like that. You've undermined my business."

"What? How? Collette's owner was happy."

"You young people swan into Dorset Hills thinking you own the place, and forget what turned us into a dog center in the first place. Classic good taste, not fads."

"That's not what I think at all."

"Well, think about this: you're on probation, young lady. From now on, I'll issue specific instructions and you'll follow them. Otherwise, good luck finding work in this town without a reference from me."

Sasha blinked back tears. She'd gone above and beyond in this shop, working overtime for weeks. There hadn't been a single complaint so far, and the dogs loved her.

The bells rang again and she turned. Framed in the doorway was a tall bald man with tattoos creeping up over the collar of his T-shirt and out from under the cuffs of his parka. His green eyes seemed all the brighter without hair for contrast. Sasha took an involuntary step backward. He was obviously in the wrong place.

"May I help you?" she asked. It crossed her mind that he might be planning to rob them. How fast could she get to the phone?

"He's here for Grover, the English bulldog," Mildred said. "Get him."

CHAPTER TWO

Sasha's spirits rose as she collected Grover from the crate in the back room. The brindle and white bulldog was an absolute sweetheart, and she'd had a lovely hour with him before Collette's appointment. Although he was only there for a bath and nail trim, the flat-faced, wrinkled dog was so obliging she'd decided to have some fun. She painted his nails black, white and silver. Then she put a silver bowtie around his neck and strapped a small black bowler under his chin with elastic. Dog costumes could be had for a song at the dollar store and it always gave owners a good laugh. The tattooed guy seemed gruff but there was no way he couldn't smile at his adorable bulldog trundling out looking like Winston Churchill. It would be a great antidote to the hit she'd taken from Millie.

Walking ahead of Grover, she came around the counter to do the big reveal. "Voila! Allow me to introduce Grover Churchill."

Grover lumbered toward Tattoos as fast as his polished spats could take him. His backside wiggled since he didn't have a tail to do the job. He was the exact opposite of everything she used to find attractive in a dog, but lately she'd begun to find beauty in all breeds. Her preference was doodle hybrids, but dogs like Grover were changing her opinion.

The man went down on one knee to greet Grover, his bald head bent over his wriggling companion. She had wondered if he was bald by choice and a dark shadow confirmed he likely had all the resources he needed for a good head of hair. As someone who cared a lot about hair—human and canine—she didn't really understand why someone would sacrifice it voluntarily. There were other ways to rebel, she figured, especially for a man in his thirties.

Finally, he looked up and his eyes had narrowed to green slits. "What did you do to my dog?"

Millie's hands shot up instantly. "It wasn't me."

The joy whooshed out of Sasha. "I thought you'd like it. It's just a costume."

"You thought I'd like seeing my bulldog look like a buffoon? His nails glitter."

"It's non-toxic and easily removed..." Her voice trailed off.

"Take off the polish, Sasha," Millie said. "Mr. Granger isn't happy with your work."

"Of course." She held out her hand for the leash. "I'm sorry, Mr. Granger."

Still on one knee, he waved her hand away. "Don't touch him. What's wrong with you people?"

"It wasn't me," Millie repeated. "I don't do costumes. They're teaching odd things in grooming school these days."

He stood and tossed Millie a glare, too. "It's your shop. I

came here because it didn't look like the ridiculous places closer to Bellington Square. But you're just Dog Town crazies like everyone else."

"Nothing could be farther from the truth," Millie said. "I've run this salon for twenty years and never polished a nail."

"You hired someone who does. And that's on you."

"Business is brisk at the holidays, Mr. Granger. A clean dog is a festive dog. So I needed temporary help. I assure you that Grover won't be decorated again."

"You got that right, because he won't be back."

Sasha looked down, blonde curls falling into her face. She tried to swallow and couldn't.

Grover left his owner and turned back to her. He pushed his head between her knees and wiggled. The bowler fell off and the bowtie twisted.

Millie leaned over the dog. "Here, let me."

Grover flinched when she touched him. His already strenuous breathing turned into a wheeze. Sasha's throat loosened and she looked up. "Stop," she said. "You're making Grover anxious. Both of you."

"Excuse me?" Their voices overlapped.

"Well, look at him. He's hiding because your voices are raised. Not because he's wearing a bowtie."

Tattoos tipped his head skeptically. "And you know so much about bulldogs?"

She shook back her hair and matched him glare for glare. "I don't know much about bulldogs, actually, but I know how to read a stressed dog. Grover was playful and confident during his grooming and now he's hiding and breathing heavily. He's not wriggling like he did when I brought him out."

"I know this dog," he said. "Grover, come here."

Grover kept his head between Sasha's knees and froze. She put her hands on her hips. "See? He's sensitive and you've upset him."

"He's sensitive because you put nail polish on him." But Tattoos looked sheepish now, and his voice softened. "Grover, come, buddy. It's okay."

"Sasha, release Mr. Granger's dog right now."

"He's not in a headlock, Millie. Let him make his own decisions."

"We don't do that here," Millie said. "Dogs don't call the shots in Dorset Hills."

"That's where you're wrong," Tattoos said. "Dogs rule this town."

"Not in my salon." Millie's voice was clipped. "Perhaps in other places." She gave Sasha a withering glance. "Newcomers have strange ideas."

"It's like a cult," Tattoos said, snapping his fingers. Grover continued to pretend his owner didn't exist.

"Why live in Dog Town if you hate the idea of it so much?" Sasha asked, genuinely curious.

He kept his eyes on the dog. "I came to Dorset Hills—not 'Dog Town'—for family reasons. I knew the place had gone nuts, but bowlers and nail polish? Honestly."

"Well, Grover seems to like it. We had a nice time. He's a very sweet dog."

"Take off his nail polish," Millie repeated.

"I don't want to wait," Tattoos said. "Just give me my dog."

Sasha didn't move. When Grover was ready to face their cynicism, he could come out on his own.

"Give him his dog, Sasha." Millie churned a hand through her bristly hair. "Now."

Bending over, Sasha murmured, "Grover, honey, your daddy wants to go."

"I am not that dog's 'daddy.' They're dogs, not babies."

"It's okay, Grover. When people are grumpy, it's not about you." She hid a grin, starting to enjoy herself. "You're the sweetest thing ever."

Grover backed up and then raised his droopy bloodshot eyes to Sasha. His square, muscular butt wriggled.

"There you go," she crooned. "What a good boy. Look at that tooth. One big toof sticking out. So cute."

"Oh my goodness gracious me. Baby talk," Tattoos said. "I'm going to be sick."

Sasha dialed it up even more. "Want to go to Daddy, Grovey?"

Grover showed no inclination to leave the sweet talk.

"Stop that," Millie said. "Let the man have his dog."

"Go to Daddy, Groves. I'll see you soon, sweetie."

"That you won't." Tattoos finally grabbed the dog's collar. As he pulled, Grover dug in his paws and then deliberately collapsed on his side.

"Maybe you should try baby talk," Sasha said, now grinning openly. "Most dogs like it. Or so I learned in grooming school."

The man was on both knees, trying to get the solid, 60-plus pound dog to stand. It was like wrestling a slick pig. Grover pretended to have no control of his muscles.

"Grover, enough," the guy said. "Let's go. Right now."

Sasha knelt, too, and said, "Up you get, baby. Time to celebrate Christmas."

Grover rolled over and started to rise.

"Thank goodess," Tattoos muttered. His eyes met Sasha's and though she expected to see fury, she saw befuddled embarrassment and a hint of something that looked like admiration.

"Is this really your dog?" she asked.

"Of course he's my dog! Why would you say that?"

She gestured to Grover, now staring up at her again. "He doesn't want to leave with you, so I just wondered if you were a walker or something."

The guy grabbed the leash and hauled on it. When Grover threatened to collapse once more, he said, "Come on, buddy. Let's run for cookies."

That worked. A stream of drool started around Grover's protruding tooth.

"There you go," Sasha said. "The key to his heart."

"How much do I owe you?" he asked Millie.

"It's on the house. I'm sorry for all this."

He hesitated for a moment, but once Grover was moving, he clearly didn't want to linger. At the door, he paused and stared back at Sasha. It may have been a trick of the light but it seemed as if he was fighting a smile. "I'll be back," he said.

After the door closed behind him, Millie shook her head. "He won't be back. So the money will come out of your pay."

"Millie, I really need that money with Petunia's spay coming up."

"Maybe you should have thought of that before you got creative with nail polish. And the way you spoke to that client was inappropriate. It's another strike against you."

"That's not fair."

"It's not enough to be good with dogs in this business. You need to be good with people, too." As she walked to one of the grooming rooms, Millie called back, "Lock the door right now and get this place cleaned up."

Sasha was turning the key when four women appeared outside. The smallest of them was carrying a mid-sized dog. Cracking open the door slightly to keep the bells from ringing, she said, "I'm sorry, we're closed."

The small woman said, "Not yet. We need help."

CHAPTER THREE

"Really, we are closed," Sasha said. "I'm afraid the owner was very insistent about that."

A woman with smooth auburn hair gave Sasha a wide smile. "Would you consider making an exception? This is a very dire situation, I'm afraid."

A taller woman whose hair was tucked into a black toque slipped her hand through the crack in the door and stilled the bells. She let the others file in and Sasha didn't resist.

"I'm Bridget Linsmore," the tall woman said, entering last with an elegant black dog at her side. "This is Beau and these are my friends, Andrea MacDuff and Nika Lothian." She pointed to the redhead first and then a woman with stunning amber eyes and curly black hair. "Cori Hogan is the one carrying the dog."

Though petite, Cori carried the dirty grey-and-white dog with ease. Her black gloves, buried deep in fur, seemed to have one neon orange finger. "We rescued this dog and it's a mess," she said. "Our usual groomer isn't available."

Sasha reached out and Cori backed away instantly. "Don't touch. She's very frightened."

"How would you expect me to groom her if I can't touch her?" she asked.

"Good point," Nika said. "What's your name?"

"Sasha Wildwood. I'm just the intern here and the owner isn't very happy with me right now. If I ask to groom this dog, she'll say no."

"Then don't ask," Cori said. "Asking gets in the way of getting things done."

"Cori, we can't jeopardize her job," Andrea said. "There must be another groomer still open."

"Not on Christmas Eve, Duff. We'll have to do it ourselves," Bridget said.

Cori shook her head. "We still have appointments and we're on call in case George is found." Her fierce, dark eyes issued a direct challenge to Sasha. "This dog has been horribly neglected. She deserves proper grooming by someone with good tools and skills."

"What breed is she?" Sasha asked. "If you know."

"Some kind of designer dog. She was..."

"In deplorable circumstances," Bridget said. "We really can't say more. But we run a dog rescue and we'll make sure this girl ends up in a good home. She's matted and will be more comfortable shaved down. There's no need for a fancy cut."

Sasha nodded. "Okay. I can't stand to see her like that."

"Shall we speak to your boss?" Duff asked.

"No," Sasha and Cori spoke over each other.

"It'll go faster if you help," Sasha told Cori. "If the rest of you could distract the owner when she comes out, maybe we could pull this off without fireworks."

Cori followed Sasha's signal, moving swiftly ahead of her into the grooming room. "What now?" she asked.

"Put the dog on the table, shut the door, and block it," Sasha said. "If the owner tries to get in, stop her. I don't want any distractions when I'm cutting so close."

"I'll keep her out." Cori set the dog on the grooming table, and flexed her hands. The two orange flares were the flipping fingers.

"Oh, sweet girl," Sasha said, running her hand lightly over the cowering dog. "You are a mess. But we'll make it all better soon."

She kept up a soothing murmur while she slipped the dog's head into the grooming noose, and then ran the clippers to get the dog used to the sound. After a minute or so, she started sheering. The hair came off the dog in one piece.

"That bad?" Cori asked.

"It's felted. Matted right down to the skin. With the new hair trapped underneath, it would have been pinching and pulling on her." The dog flinched again. "There are a couple of sores, but they'll heal quickly once the fur is gone. Who could do something like this?"

Cori paced back and forth by the door. "You'd be surprised what people do. It's easier not to know."

There were voices outside. Millie had come out to discover the women. "Stand guard," Sasha told Cori. "It won't take long to clip but I also want to do her nails and give her a quick bath."

She heard Duff's light laughter and knew she was trying to charm Millie. It was unlikely to be successful. In her five weeks there, she'd never seen Millie charmed. She wasn't a horrible woman; her love for dogs was genuine and that meant she couldn't be all bad. But she seemed to have lost her way with humans.

Luckily the dog was quiet to the point of apathy. She didn't protest at the clippers, even when Sasha buzzed with lightning speed down each foreleg, across the belly, and down the hind legs. The tail she buzzed to the bare rat tail she'd been horrified to see with Maxwell, the goldendoodle, earlier. Her standards had changed quickly from frills to functionality. Snap-snap-snap went the clippers on overgrown claws. Bits shot out like shrapnel and Cori ducked after being struck in the cheek.

"Holy crap, you need danger pay," she said.

Turning on the water, Sasha tested it to make sure the temperature was just right and then whisked the dog into the tub. "What's her name?" she asked.

"Doesn't have one yet. We rename them to give them a fresh start."

"Opal," Sasha said, lathering the dog. "She seems like a real gem. So quiet."

"That's because she's terrified. She'll get her spark back."

After a few moments, the dog lifted her face to the spray. "There you go," Sasha said. "You're going to be a pretty girl when this grows out."

Cori backed against the door to avoid the spray. Suddenly the doorknob turned and Millie's voice rang out. "Sasha Wildwood! What are you doing in there?"

"Just a quick bath. Be done in two shakes of a lamb's tail." It was an expression Millie used herself.

"Tell me this isn't some filthy rescue on my premises, Sasha. It could be covered in fleas and infest the real clients."

"I'll scrub the room down thoroughly, like always."

"I want that dog out of here right now. I'm coming in."

Cori applied her shoulder to the door, cursing quietly.

"Just give me a minute, Millie," Sasha called again. "Almost done."

"How are you— Wait a second, do you have someone else in there?" Millie pushed harder. "It's that nasty little rescuer isn't it? The one everyone's talking about."

Cori smirked to confirm it. Millie continued to push and Cori continued to push and it went on that way for another few minutes while Sasha got the dog out of the tub and toweled off. "Millie, I am not sending this dog out into winter without drying her. Whatever you're worried about, the damage is done."

There was silence at the other side of the door. "Yes, it is. When you're finished, grab your things, because you're fired."

"I'M SO SORRY, SASHA," Bridget said as she drove her home in her battered lime-green van.

Sasha sat in the back between Nika and Duff, with the dog on her lap wrapped up in a fluffy blanket. "Don't be. Millie wanted to fire me anyway. She didn't like my attitude."

"If it's any consolation, we love your attitude," Duff said.

"Agreed," Bridget and Nika said in unison.

"I'm reserving judgment," Cori said, from the passenger seat. "You delayed saying yes about three minutes too long."

"She's a hard woman to please," Sasha said to Nika.

Nika laughed. "You have no idea. But she likes you. Otherwise, you wouldn't get to hold the dog."

"If only we'd had a good hour," Sasha said. "The poor thing is traumatized."

"But she'll feel so much better soon," Bridget said. "You'd be surprised at dogs' resilience. Within a week she'll be playing in our yards with the other dogs. Maybe she'll be part of my Thanksgiving Rescue Pageant next year. But I doubt I'll be able to hold onto her that long. She deserves a real home soon."

"I wish I could take her but I have my hands full with Tuni," Sasha said.

"Tuni?" Bridget asked, as she parked the van in front of Sasha's place.

"Petunia. My Welsh springer spaniel. She's just turned a year and she's so high energy."

Cori snorted. "What do you expect from a sporting dog? She's bred to run the fields all day long. It was a silly choice for a personal pet."

"It wasn't my choice," Sasha said. "But I love her and I'm making the best of it."

Something in her tone made Cori's mouth snap shut. Bridget pinched her arm to keep it that way, and said, "I'm sure she's lovely, Sasha. Now, what can we do to help you get another job?"

"You don't need to rescue me, too," Sasha said. "I'll be fine. I finished my grooming certification two weeks ago and surely someone will be hiring."

The women all looked at each other. A silent communication must have taken place because they all seemed to be on the same page when Duff spoke. "Have you considered running your own business?"

"Me? On my own? Definitely not. I'm the type of person who likes a boss."

"Are you sure about that?" Bridget asked. "Because you seemed like the type of person who likes to make her own decisions."

"And tell her boss to shove it," Cori said.

"Cori, stop," Duff said.

"What? It's a compliment."

"That was an unusual situation," Sasha said. "I'd had a couple of run-ins with Millie earlier."

"Where you told her to shove it?" Cori asked, snickering.

Sasha thought about it. "I guess so. She rubs me the wrong way. I never had a moment's trouble working for people in hair salons for ten years before that."

"Outside of Dog Town," Bridget said. "The place changes you."

"You get to become who you really are," Cori said.

Duff tipped her head of beautiful auburn hair. "No pressure, Sasha, but if you're looking to branch out, we can help."

"I wouldn't have a clue how to start my own business."

"You'd start by finding a storefront," Duff said. "Which I could handle, because I'm a real estate agent."

"Then we'd help you get clients," Bridget said. "Our friend Maisie Todd is a great groomer but she's been swamped since my last pageant. You could take some of her overflow."

"Arianna Torrance is cutting back on grooming, too," Nika said. "She wants to focus more on her breeding business. Plus I can send referrals from the vet practice where I work."

"That would give you a good start," Duff said.

"I don't know," Sasha said. "I don't have the tools I need. It would be a couple of thousand to set up properly."

"Maybe we could do a fundraiser," Nika said.

"I have enough," Sasha said. "Barely. My vet bills have been awful this year. Tuni had a rare viral infection. She's only now in good enough shape to be spayed. And that's another expense."

"I'm a vet technician," Nika said. "I can get you a deal on the spay."

Sasha stared around at them. "You're all so kind. I—I haven't found it all that easy to make my way in Dorset Hills."

"There's a long onboarding process for newcomers," Duff said. "It's like 'Survivor,' only with dogs."

"Retraining was a good call," Bridget said. "You'll blend better with a dog speciality."

"How about we check out what space is available over the holidays and take it from there?" Duff asked. "If there's nothing available, you can start looking for regular jobs."

"Millie implied she'd badmouth me. Even though clients were happy."

"Those are the clients you'll poach," Cori said, grinning. "It'll be fun."

Sasha sat silently, stroking the dog's damp, bristly head. "I never saw myself as an entrepreneur."

"Most of us don't," Cori said. "Until we piss off so many people we have no choice but to run our own show."

"And that's when we really succeed," Bridget said.

"It's how I became the best dog trainer in town," Cori said. She was matter-of-fact and everyone else nodded in agreement.

"Do you really want to groom under the old guard like Millie Trowbridge?" Nika asked. "I've seen her running with her poodle, all puffs and pompoms."

"She says a classic poodle cut is a walking advertisement," Sasha said.

"Not in Dorset Hills," Duff said. "Not anymore. You

need to be light on your feet. Ready to follow trends. Or better yet, set them."

"Listen to Duff," Bridget said. "She's a makeover expert. Without her guidance my Thanksgiving pageant would have been a bust this year. I didn't want to change, but the town has. And if I can, anyone can."

Still Sasha hesitated. "That's my life savings, really. I live in a basement apartment and spent the rest on the grooming course. If it fails—"

"If it fails, there's a Plan B," Duff said. "We don't give up on dogs or good people."

"Emphasis on the 'good,'" Cori said. "We give up on losers all the time." She craned around the seat and grinned at Sasha. "Give the dog to Nika. Opal, you said?"

"She let you name the dog?" Nika asked. "It took me a year to earn that privilege."

"I'll be in touch about space next week," Duff said. "Merry Christmas."

"But—"

The sliding door opened and Duff gave her a little shove. "It was great—"

The last word was cut off as the van sped away.

CHAPTER FOUR

Tuni went into her usual frenzy as Sasha walked down the stairs to her basement apartment. The upper half of the door was mottled glass and she could see a faint dark shape hurtling into view and then dropping out of sight again. The dog seemed to be on springs. Maybe that's where the "springer" in the breed name came from.

"Down, Tuni," she said, pushing the door open. "Sit."

It was a struggle for the dog, but she did it and her whole body quivered from the effort. She had smooth brown and white fur with glorious full feathers underneath. Her muzzle was long, delicate, and dotted with freckles, and her eyes were bright and alert. It was like Tuni was desperately trying to intuit her thoughts. The dog was wrong more often than she was right, but there was no doubt her intentions were good. When she matured, she'd be perfect.

Not that Sasha was entirely sure what perfect looked like. Tuni was the first dog she'd ever owned. At this point, there was definitely room for improvement, especially in the evenings, when Tuni had pent-up energy. She got a good run in the morning, and was let out twice by the landlord during the day. Still, the pup was wound up pretty tight by the time Sasha got home.

Grabbing the leash, she took Tuni outside immediately. There would be no peace and joy on Christmas Eve until the dog chased a ball in the park for awhile.

Sasha doubted there was much joy in store for her at all, after what had happened that day. She walked briskly down the well-lit street. Her apartment was a little dungeon but at least she lived in a great part of town. It was just a half-hour walk to Bellington Square and the neighborhood parks were excellent.

The local fenced dog park was nearly empty when she arrived. Unlike her, most people had plans for Christmas Eve. When she'd moved to Dorset Hills, dogs were the primary attraction, but Christmas was a close second. She had been looking forward to the holidays since spring, when Dog Town looked like her happily-ever-after. But then everything fell apart. Lawrence, her fiancé, had left town by summer, and now she was spending the holiday hurling a glow-in-the-dark ball across a fenced yard.

Tuni was usually insatiable when it came to fetch but tonight she wore out before Sasha did. Finally Tuni flopped on top of the ball so that Sasha couldn't throw it again.

"Done already?" Sasha asked. Her aching shoulder suggested more time had passed than she realized. She hadn't even noticed that fat flakes of snow had started to fall.

Heading for the gate, she turned and sat abruptly on a bench. The adrenaline drained out of her suddenly and the effects of the day kicked in. What had she just done? All her working life she'd been a model employee, beloved by her bosses, colleagues and clients. How had she managed to get herself fired? She had no desire to start her own business. But with a bad reference from Mildred Trowbridge, her name would be mud in the grooming community. Clients would be easier to find than a new employer.

Tuni rested her long muzzle on Sasha's thigh and whined. The dog often sensed her moods before Sasha even knew them herself. She tried to keep up a good front because it wasn't fair to put Tuni through the wringer, too. They'd both had a hard year with health challenges and loss. But she was the leader here.

"It's okay, my girl. Things are just going to change for us again." She stroked the dog's long plumy ears and smiled. "And this time it won't suck. I mean, it might. I might lose what little savings I have. I might embarrass myself even more than I did today. But there's an upside, and you know what that is?" Tuni waved her tail hopefully. "The upside is that you can come to work with me. I never wanted to leave you alone, but Mean Millie didn't want you at her shop. Now, you can be the star at mine. How about that?"

Now Tuni's tail beat steadily, like a metronome. Whatever his failings, Lawrence had worked hard to find a breeder willing to leave her tail intact. It was still commonplace to dock the tails of hunting dogs like spaniels, but a dog without its rightful tail was just wrong, she'd always thought. Not that a Welsh springer had been her first choice, or even her 30th. Lawrence had made that choice, as he'd made most others. But in this case, at least, it had come out well.

Ironically, it was Tuni's typical breed traits that had frustrated Lawrence, especially the relentlessly high energy. So when he packed up his things, Tuni was not among them. Sasha hadn't needed to fight for her, although she would have. Lawrence could break her heart, he could destroy all her hopes and dreams, but he could not take the dog she'd fallen for. Because of Tuni, she wasn't even bitter.

Well, barely.

"Hello, young lady."

Shuffling through the gate was Bartholomew Barnes, and his shaggy old crossbreed, Puck. He'd adopted Puck from a shelter nearly 10 years earlier, and claimed to have no idea of the dog's heritage. It would have been easier to guess if he'd kept Puck properly groomed, but both of them looked perpetually scruffy. Bart's dark coat had been fine once, and Puck's probably had, too. Two old men couldn't be bothered with vanities, he said.

"Hey, Bart. Merry Christmas to you and Puck."

He eased himself down, using his cane. "What's a pretty girl like you doing here alone on Christmas Eve?"

"Same reason you're here, I guess," she said.

"You're too crusty for polite society?"

She laughed. "Maybe so. I *was* crusty today, and I got myself fired for it."

His pale eyes glittered behind round wire glasses. "I told you to watch that lip, didn't I?"

"You did. And I didn't." She watched as Tuni fluttered around Puck, trying without success to get his attention. The old dog found her energy offensive and gave her an occasional nip to remind her of that. "I used to keep quiet. After Lawrence left my tongue got loose."

"Lawrence," he said, as if the word tasted tart. "Good riddance to him."

"Right? That's how I see it. At least, I do now."

"Does he send money, at least? What kind of man leaves a woman when—"

"It's all right, Bart. I can take care of myself. And Tuni. I'm just going to have to get creative."

"He uprooted your life and brought you here."

"True, but I chose to stay when he left. My sister wanted me to come to San Francisco."

Bart made a semicircle in the snow with his cane. "No snow in San Francisco. And plenty of dogs, from what I hear."

She looked up and let snowflakes fall into her face. "Dog Town was too small for Lawrence. It's just right for me."

Lawrence had hated Dorset Hills so much he refused to unpack. He said it was overrated and absurd. Meanwhile, the town got its eyeteeth into Sasha and wouldn't let go. It was like their new setting revealed how little they truly had in common. She'd just never noticed it out in the "real world."

"This town's getting too big for its own good," Bart said, shaking his head. "Dorset Hills used to have horse sense. Now everyone has an agenda. You'll need to be careful, young lady."

Somehow it didn't bother her when Bart called her that. It sounded fond, instead of patronizing.

"I know. Especially if I open my own grooming salon. I already have so many ideas."

"Girls with big ideas can get in trouble around here." Reaching into his pocket, he pulled out a candy cane and offered it to her. "But I imagine it'll work out just fine."

She accepted the candy cane and peeled off the plastic wrapper. "I would love for Puck to be my first customer."

He dismissed the idea with a wave. "Puck is fine as he is."

"Bart, I'm sorry, but Puck's a mess. He's overgrown and shaggy. I can't even tell if he's black or brown."

"Does it matter?" His glasses slipped down and he eyed

her over the rims. "We're comfortable. Don't try to fix men, young lady. It never ends well."

"I'm not trying to fix you—er, Puck. Just tidy him up."

He took the candy cane out of her hand. "No sweets for meddlers."

"Fine. Never mind then."

She held out her hand and he gave the candy cane back.

"Just relax and let things unfold as they're meant to," he said, using his cane to push himself up. "It works better that way."

"That's not in my nature. I'm a doer." She got up and followed him out of the enclosed dog area and into the park proper. "I'll need to be a doer to get a business running."

Bart shrugged. "Let the business run to you. Push too hard and you'll regret it. Mark my words."

There was a shout from the main trail and Sasha turned. A woman with a beagle on a leash was running toward her. "Is that a Welsh springer spaniel?" she called.

Sasha shouted back, "Yes," and Bart covered one ear with his free hand.

"Oh my gosh, I've never seen one in real life," the woman said. "This is so exciting. Would you mind if I took a picture?"

Sasha stopped walking despite Bart's grumbled complaints. When the woman reached her, she said, "You're Remi Malone. We met this afternoon."

Remi and her friend Flynn Strathmore had come into the salon to see if the bulletin board had posters for dogs in need of new homes.

"Yes! Sasha, right? We didn't find a dog for Flynn's husband, I'm afraid," Remi said, wiping the snow off her phone and taking Tuni's picture.

The puffy flakes were getting thicker, almost guaranteeing the white Christmas everyone craved. A thaw earlier in the week had worried the entire town.

A tall man joined them, and Remi slipped her arm through his. "This is my boyfriend, Tiller Iverson." She jiggled the leash. "And my other boyfriend, Leo."

"Wow, I came first in the introductions tonight," Tiller said, grinning. "I guess she's angling for a Christmas present."

Remi smiled up at Tiller and for a moment Sasha felt as if she were intruding. The couple seemed to be caught in their own magical snow globe, and it gave her a pang. But Remi snapped out of it quickly and introduced herself to Bart and Puck. The latter gave an air snap at Leo, and the dog reeled back between Remi's boots. Tuni came forward eagerly to make nice however, and there was much wagging and sniffing between the two spotted dogs.

"I assume you're on your way to the Craven Road party?" Remi asked.

Sasha shook her head. "Never heard of it."

"Oh, you'll love it. Come with us, if you can spare an hour or two."

"Well, I have to—"

There was a sharp poke between her shoulder blades from a cane. "Go on, young lady. Puck and I can see ourselves home."

"Perfect," Remi said. "If you're a sucker for Christmas like I am, you're in for a treat."

Sasha jolted forward from another jab from Bart's cane. "You could come along, Bart," she said. "The more the merrier."

"I'll be with you in spirit," he said, stumping off.

CHAPTER FIVE

Sasha thought she knew the neighborhood well, but she'd somehow missed Craven Road. Perhaps Craven Road wanted to be missed, or maybe it magically disappeared unless you had an open invitation, like Remi. As they turned the corner, it was as if they had entered Santa's secret village.

"Oh my goodness how pretty." The words tumbled out of Sasha's mouth in a rush. "Is this for real?"

"For real," Remi said, smiling. "It's one of the seven wonders of Dog Town."

"Do I know the other five?" Tiller asked. "Assuming you're one of them."

Sasha laughed at that. "He's good, isn't he?"

"The best." Remi stood on tiptoes to kiss Tiller's cheek. "My evergreen high school sweetheart."

They started down the road of wonder. It truly was like stepping out of Dog Town, because none of the city's unofficial rules about seasonal decorating seemed to apply on this street. Council endorsed a simple elegant look, specifically strings of clear lights wrapped around pine boughs and a few silver bows. Sasha had been surprised when the decorations went up around town in early December and there was hardly a colored bulb to be seen.

Craven Road didn't get the memo. Here, there was color... lots of it. And yet, it wasn't a jangly riot. Every house had lights, but the owners must have consulted one another, because the colors flowed seamlessly, like carefully selected jewels. There were six massive pines on the strip, each circled right up to the top in multicolored lights.

"Ooohh." Sasha tipped her head back. "Pretty."

"The fire department comes over and puts them up," Remi said. "And everyone pretends they didn't."

"There's more going on under the surface of Dog Town than I knew," Sasha said.

"Only lifers like me know the half of it," Remi said, tugging her arm. "Come on. We don't want to miss the food."

At every house, residents offered treats of one kind or another, and by the time she was halfway down the street Sasha was full. There was none of the garish vulgarity City Council feared, such as sky-high inflatable snowmen. Instead there were pretty ornaments and angels—lots of angels. The fence on one side of the road was covered in unique and festive artwork. Children's laughter rose in the air, along with barking. Most the dogs were unleashed, and behaved.

"This is the best Christmas ever," Sasha said, only partially influenced by the spiked eggnog. "I love Dog Town."

Remi gave her a curious look, but all she said was, "Wait till you hear the carolling. It's better than the City choir. Rebels have the best voices."

At the far end of the street, people had gathered in a

circle. A flawless soprano voice rose in "What Child is This." Tears came to Sasha's eyes and she blinked rapidly to clear them. What would Remi and Tiller think if she bawled during carols?

"Could you hold Leo?" Remi asked, passing the dog to Sasha.

"Sure." The small beagle relaxed against her chest and let out a sigh. Then he gazed up at her and whined.

"He wants to be patted," Remi prompted.

"When doesn't he?" Tiller muttered. "We need help or our hands will fall off from overuse."

"Oh stop, Mr. Grinch," Remi said. "Listen to the music."

Sasha continued to pat Leo through another couple of carols and by the time the singers launched into "Jingle Bell Rock," she was laughing. Leo politely let her know he was ready to get down and tussle with Tuni again. "Is he a therapy dog?" she asked Remi.

"Yep, and he's turned my life around," Remi said. "You know what will turn *yours* around? The house at the end of the street has the best fruitcake. You can get drunk off the smell. Let's hurry or we'll miss it."

When they got there, people were sitting around the lawn on chairs and crates, while kids tried hard to build a snowman from trampled snow.

"Well, if it isn't lady twinkle toes," a man's voice said, behind Sasha.

She turned curiously just as a chunky English bulldog pushed his head between her shins.

"Grover! Hey buddy!" She knelt in the snow and he wriggled around, trying to lick her face. Tuni muscled in and the force of two excited dogs pushed Sasha over into the slushy snow on the street. "Tuni, leave it," she said, shielding her face from the roughhousing.

Two gloved hands came down and seized Grover's collar. Tattoos were visible between the gloves and the cuffs. "Leave it," he echoed.

Grover had no intention of leaving it. He crawled into Sasha's lap as she sat in the slush and Tuni climbed on top of him. Tuni's wet tail whipped into Sasha's eyes, blinding her for a moment. "Ow, ow, ow."

There was a flurry and then a vacuum as Tuni disappeared from the equation. When her vision cleared, Sasha saw that Tiller had picked Tuni up and cradled her in his arms. "Settle down, now," he said. "I know all about party girls like you. That's why I left Roxy at home tonight."

Remi kept Leo well back from the fray, and Grover's owner crouched beside Sasha. He started to reach out for his dog, then stopped. "May I?"

It was decent of him to ask, because Grover had settled his 60 pounds quite deliberately into her lap, and extricating him would take the type of manoeuvring that usually required an invitation, if not a wedding ring.

"Let me," she said. Moving Grover on her own was like grappling with a bowling ball. Pushing with both hands against the dog's broad chest, she eased herself backwards. Before he could stage a new assault she quickly got to her feet. The back of her coat and her mittens were soaked and muddy.

She stuck one wet hand out. "Sasha Wildwood."

"Griffin Granger," he said, shaking it.

"You live here?" she asked. "On magical Craven Road?"

"Just visiting with friends. They claim you can get drunk off the fruitcake." He smiled and his expression thawed so much that he looked like a different man. A handsome and friendly man. He must have been into the fruitcake already.

Remi came forward, hand outstretched. Her job as a fundraiser for the hospital seemed to have made her confident. "Grover is so cute," she said. "I absolutely love his nails. The silver catches all the lights."

Griffin's smile faded. "I can see why you two are friends."

"I just met Sasha today, actually," Remi said, introducing herself and Tiller. "But I know good people when I see them."

"She does," Tiller agreed. "We gather friends and dogs like a snowball rolling downhill. And I love it."

Remi beamed up at him. It was another one of those private-in-public moments. This time, Sasha's heart twanged even harder, remembering what she'd lost—or worse, never had. She turned to Griffin and found him staring at the lovebirds, too.

Snapping out of it, he directed green eyes at her. They didn't look as exotic now that a bulky grey wool hat covered his buzzed head. "I'm sorry Grover knocked you over," he said. "He's very strong."

"My coat will dry." She patted her streaming eyes with a tissue. "My sight might not recover from getting whacked by my own dog's tail."

"What kind of dog is she?" He looked at Tuni, who was lolling in Tiller's arms as he chatted to the new people Remi was gathering. Leo was loose, working his charm among the boots.

"A Welsh springer spaniel," she said.

"Huh. I didn't picture that."

Don't ask, don't ask, don't ask, she told herself and then, "What exactly did you picture?"

"Froufrou," he said. "Obviously. Powder puffs and pink tutus. Doesn't a girl like you want a doggie daughter to dress up?"

Annoyance flared in her gut. "A girl like me? What do you know about me?"

He shrugged and gave a little smirk. "Dorset Hills is full of people like you who turn dogs into dolls. Why don't I see silver nail polish on *your* dog?"

She tamped down her anger. Why give him the satisfaction? "Because a groomer's dog goes barefoot, of course. Tuni's my last priority when I'm beautifying other people's dogs all day."

"Beautifying being a relative term."

Grover ambled over and stuck his head between her shins again. It was his signature move. Griffin pressed his lips together, which told her the move irritated him. He wanted Grover to dislike her, too. Stubborn Grover had a mind of his own.

"Well, I won't be beautifying any dogs for awhile, thanks to you. Your mantrum over a little dog bling got me fired today."

His eyes widened. "What?"

"Mildred read me the riot act for talking back to you. Now I'm jobless. So Merry Christmas."

"That was a total overreaction." His eyes darted all over to avoid looking at her.

"Agreed. All I did was put a bowtie and a bowler on your dog. Hardly a crime."

"It was the polish that did it," he muttered. "And I meant Mildred overreacted. She didn't need to fire you for being silly."

"Silly? Well, I'll certainly be more selective about my peticures from now on."

His eyes landed back on her. "For someone who got fired, you don't sound all that upset. Are you having me on?"

"Nope. I'm banned for life from the Pewter Poodle. Why on earth did you bring Grover to a place with a name like that if you have a nail polish phobia?"

"It was close to my job site and the only appointment I could get on short notice."

She shrugged. "My lucky day, I guess."

A massive black bouvier came barrelling across the street and Leo was right in his path. Before anyone else could move, Griffin bent and scooped up the beagle. "That was close, little buddy," he said. When he tried to pass the dog to Remi, Leo went limp and snuggled under Griffin's chin. All the man's rough edges melted then and he blinked a few times in abject surrender.

"Another one bites the dust," Tiller said, laughing at Griffin's expression. "Welcome to Leo's pack."

Tiller put Tuni down and she rushed over to Grover and started roughhousing. The big bulldog couldn't keep up, but he clearly enjoyed it.

"Tuni looks familiar," Griffin said, watching her. "Are there a lot of them in town?"

"As far as I know, she's the only Welshie around."

"Oh. You're one of those."

Don't ask. Don't ask. Don't ask. "One of those *what*?"

"One of those Dog Towners who has to have a rare dog to stand out."

Now she really was angry and the words popped out like firecrackers. "First you contributed to getting me fired and then you diss my choice in dogs?"

Grover put his head back between her shins and even irrepressible Tuni froze.

"Contributed?" Griffin was all over the word. "So there were other reasons you got fired?"

She moved her right foot so that Grover was exposed. "Look, your dog likes me, so obviously I did a pretty good job. And you didn't pay a cent for it, either. So, if you'll excuse me, I'm going to get some of that famous fruitcake."

"I ate the last piece," he said, grinning as he bent to leash Grover.

Sasha shook her head. "Of course you did."

As she turned away, he said, "I'm sorry about your job. Really."

Tuni pulled back to Grover, and the bulldog strained on the leash to follow Sasha. "It's not the worst thing that happened to me this year. Not by a long shot."

"Listen," he called after her. "Can we talk about your dog for a second?"

There was nothing he could say about Tuni that would interest her.

"No," she said, trudging away. "But Merry Christmas. Hope Santa is good to Grover."

CHAPTER SIX

The little shop on Main Street was dim and dingy, but the cheery voices and smiling faces made it seem bright. It was the third place they'd checked out that afternoon and she was enjoying spending time with Duff, Bridget, Cori and Nika more than the actual mission of finding salon space.

Christmas on her own had been surprisingly peaceful, and Tuni gave her a reason to resist her sister's arm-twisting to fly away from Dog Town. Instead, she'd spent the time hiking, volunteering and attending dog-friendly activities. She'd proven to herself that she could be happy on her own, but vowed next Christmas would be different. It all started here, with new acquaintances and potential friends.

With a sweep of her arm, Duff asked, "It's perfect, am I right?"

It was far from perfect, Sasha thought, although the location was great. The shop was on the older end of Main, which hadn't fully transitioned from the stodgy "old" Dorset Hills to the revitalized Dog Town. Some businesses had turned over, already. Across the street, the former shoe repair had become Crackers, the vegan dog bakery. On this side, however, Bertucci's Fine Italian Meats huddled up with Harvester Produce and shot disapproving looks at the new retail kids in town.

"It's going to take some work," Sasha said. "And money."

"Can't be that bad," Nika said, spinning on a cracked brown faux leather swivel chair in front of one of the twin mirrors. "It's a hair salon. That's just like a groomer, no?"

Sasha laughed. "Well, they both have sinks, I guess. Even a modern salon would be a big transition. Carole's Curls is pretty outdated."

"I used to get my hair cut here when I was a kid," Remi said, coming through the door with Leo. "It's barely changed."

"And it wouldn't have changed if Carole hadn't tripped over her dog and shattered her leg," Duff said. "She said she might never stand again, and needs out of the lease quickly. That's the only way we'd get a storefront on Main. It's like a Christmas miracle."

"Not for Carole," Cori said.

"Not for Carole," Duff agreed. "It's a shame, but this will free up money she needs for recovery. If she wants to work again, I can help her get a new space."

Sasha touched the other styling chair and sighed. "Isn't it bad karma to steal a space out from under a sick lady?"

"It's not your fault," Bridget said. "I feel bad for her, too, but she decided to put the shop up for lease. If you don't grab it, someone else will."

Beau stepped forward and inspected Sasha carefully. He sniffed her bare hands and her boots, seemingly taking inventory. She wasn't sure how to interpret the verdict, but the waving tail suggested a "pass." He returned to Bridget's side and it was as if they had a secret communication. She nodded in agreement, as if he'd spoken.

Sending the empty chair in a spin, Sasha ran her fingers along the equipment on the shelves. Scissors, combs, brushes, curling irons, dryers, lotions and potions. It was all familiar of course... the tools of her former trade.

"Feeling nostalgic?" Bridget asked.

"Maybe a little." She smiled at Bridget in the mirror. "Can I be honest?"

Bridget gave her a wry smile. "I expect nothing else."

"Your hair is a bit uneven. Did you cut it yourself?"

All of the women laughed, especially Cori. "Maisie took grooming shears to her before the pageant," she said.

"It looked great at the time," Duff said.

Sasha patted the chair. "Sit. I like to cut dry, and I haven't lost my touch, I promise."

Scissors in hand, she remembered what she'd liked best about her old job—the camaraderie. She'd left nearly a hundred disappointed clients behind when Lawrence got the notion to trade Boston for Dorset Hills. It had seemed crazy to others, but she was ready for a big change and more than ready for a dog. Their small condo had made dog ownership challenging. At least, that's what Lawrence had balked over. Turned out space was the least of his worries.

Everyone else chatted as she worked, and she took it in without losing her focus. She was nowhere near that zen stage with grooming, and probably never would be. Dogs were too unpredictable. By the time she was done, Bridget looked fresh and stylish.

Nika raised her hand. "Me, me!"

Her long, heavy curls offered a new challenge. Circling the chair, Sasha poked with the long end of the comb and pondered. Finally she made strategic vertical snips that made everything fall into order.

"Wow," Nika said, raising her hands. "I'm gorgeous."

"That you are," Sasha said. "Touch little. Wash seldom. Brush never. Treat these curls like fragile china."

"Fragile china," Nika repeated, getting up. "Your turn," she told Duff. "She's a master."

"I hate to mix business and haircuts," Duff said. "But are we closing this deal or not?"

Sasha looked around at the five eager faces. She didn't want to disappoint them, but it all felt so daunting. Last year had been exhausting, and now, on January 2nd, the new year looked just as daunting.

Remi must have sensed her conflict, because Leo, the therapy dog, struggled to get down from her arms. He walked over to Sasha, put his paws on her shin and waited to be lifted into her arms. He calmed her in a way Tuni couldn't, at least, not yet. One day, with more training, maybe they could achieve this, too.

"We'll all help, Sasha," Remi said. "Tiller, too. He's great with his hands."

"How great?" Nika asked, smirking.

"About as great as Sullivan, likely," Bridget said, when Remi's face flooded with color. "What about you and that dog cop, Nika? I haven't heard his name in a while."

Nika returned to the other chair and kicked her legs. "I gave him up. For the Mafia."

The Mafia? Sasha's curiosity was piqued, but she decided to stay quiet and let things play out. Hairstylists learned a lot that way.

"What?" Remi asked. "That seems extreme."

"Good call," Cori said. "He's with the police force now,

and we can't have cops all over us. What if Nika talked in her sleep?"

"At some point it might have become a conflict of interest," Bridget said. "Given how often the Rescue Mafia bends the law. I'm sorry it didn't work out, Nika, but you'll meet someone else soon."

Sasha glanced from one to another and wondered how exactly they bent the law. Everyone seemed to be in on the secret but her.

"Nika, I have a great idea," Remi said. "Volunteer with me for the Valentine's Day event. We can find you the most eligible bachelor in town and raise money for service dogs at the same time."

"I know an invitation to slave labor when I hear it," Nika said. "I already give generously to this town through the Thanksgiving pageant. But this sounds right up Sasha's ally."

Sasha held up her scissors. "I'll be busy enough getting this place started, won't I?"

The comment was definitive enough for Duff. "Let's lock this place down," she said, fingers flying on her phone.

"Joining the Valentine's committee is a good idea, Sasha," Bridget said. "They need a groomer for the dogs. You could show your chops and meet potential clients. If you want, I'll put in a good word with my rep at the city."

"What about your friend Maisie? Doesn't she want the gig?"

"She's away on a cruise with her family," Bridget said. "And she doesn't need more exposure right now."

Cori crossed her arms, orange flares curled over the sleeves of her parka. "But does Sasha really have the grooming chops?"

Rising to the challenge, Sasha slapped the empty chair. "Sit down and I'll show you."

"With dogs, I mean. All we saw was you shaving Opal down to the bone."

"Which she did with admirable speed and composure," Duff said. "Then she lost her job for it, remember."

Nika and Duff grabbed Cori's shoulders and pressed her into the swivel chair. "Give this one a trim," Nika said. "She thinks getting her hair cut is frivolous when there are so many dogs in need in this town."

"It is frivolous," Cori said, squirming. "I'd grow it out but it would take even more time—time I could be spending on those dogs in need."

Sasha appraised Cori in the mirror. "You'll be glad to hear I do a mean Audrey Hepburn cut. She was a leader in animal rescue, right?"

"Don't waste your sweet talk on me," Cori said, trying to get out of the chair. Duff and Nika restrained her. "This is stupid."

"You told me to show you my chops," Sasha said. "And I'm chopping." She snipped a big chunk out of Cori's hair, and took her hostage. "Now, stay. Stay."

"Never repeat a command," Cori said. "Say it once and mean it. Repeating shows weakness."

"Quiet," Sasha said. Just once.

Then she cut Cori's hair into a precise yet feminine cut. "You have great bone structure."

Cori rolled her eyes. "Audrey Hepburn scissor wizardry won't get you far in this town."

Sasha plucked her tablet from her purse. "Voila. My portfolio."

Holding it out for everyone to see, she flipped through

two dozen grooming shots, ending with several angles on Collette, the goldendoodle.

"Beautiful," Remi said. "She looks like a Muppet."

"Exactly." Sasha smiled. "You get me. You really get me. Unlike Mildred. My Muppet Aesthetic was the first strike against me the day I got fired."

The women looked at each other in another silent consultation, and as usual Duff found the words. "You'll do very well in Dorset Hills, Sasha. Appearances count more than ever around this town. You can build a brand around this look, and people will be lining up at the door with their dogs."

Sasha brightened. "I hope so. Millie said newfangled didn't fly around here."

"Old school," Duff said. "And while our resistance to change nearly burned us with the pageant, you can use our experience to bolster your business."

"By 'us' she means me," Bridget said.

"Cori, too," Duff said.

"Go ahead and cater to the idiots," Cori muttered, angling her head this way and that to check out her hair. "Leave me out of it."

"You look beautiful, Cori," Duff said.

"Whatever." Cori brushed the hair out of her collar, orange fingers flashing. "It itches."

"You're welcome," Sasha said, reaching for a fluffy brush and swishing it over the back of Cori's neck. "All haircuts and dog grooming on the house for my backers."

Duff and Bridget exchanged another significant look. "We're going to do everything we can to get you launched," Duff said. "But there's something you should know..."

"Does it have anything to do with this Mafia business?" Sasha asked.

Cori raised her orange flares and hissed for silence.

"Paranoid much?" Nika asked.

"Walls have ears," Cori said. "With the mayor's new dog court farce underway, we should all be extra cautious."

"She's right," Duff said. "Marti Forrester's a nice person who's up to her armpits in political alligators. We do need to be careful, at least within city limits."

Bridget waited for everyone to simmer down before speaking. "Sasha, the term Rescue Mafia is facetious but our work isn't. You saw the results on Christmas Eve, with Opal, and we helped recover Mim Gardiner's dog, George, too. Sometimes we do bend the law, and we're not as far under the radar as we used to be."

"In other words, it's probably wise to pretend you don't know too much about our work," Duff said. "At least until you get a solid clientele."

"Understood," Sasha said. "As long as you understand how grateful I am for your help."

Duff rooted around in her big leather handbag and pulled out a bottle of sparkling wine. Nika gleefully popped the cork and they dusted off Carole's old mugs to toast the success of the new doggie salon.

"Do you have a name in mind?" Remi asked.

Sasha nodded. "The Model Dog."

"To Model Dogs," Bridget said, passing the bottle.

"Remi, sit," Sasha said. "That bob is looking a bit dated."

"No Muppeting please," Remi said.

"Trust me," Sasha said. "If Cori did, anyone can."

CHAPTER SEVEN

Sasha hurried through Bellington Square toward City Hall on the way to the Valentine's Day planning committee meeting. Her coat was unzipped, although the day was as wintry as it should be on January 10th. When she was nervous, she overheated, and the last thing she wanted was to arrive sweaty and flushed. Pausing in front of towering twin bronze German shepherds, she looked up and smiled. When she'd arrived in Dorset Hills, none of the statues that dotted the town's landscape existed. The first was unveiled at the Barton Gallery of Art on Labor Day weekend and now they were popping up everywhere. Unlike a lot of people—especially the old guard—Sasha absolutely loved them. For starters, they helped a newcomer navigate around town easily. But they also conveyed the quirky charm she loved about her adopted home. Her only complaint was that she'd likely never see a Welsh Springer spaniel make an appearance. To the untrained eye, all bronze spaniels probably looked the same.

Her excitement built as she ran up the wide stairs of City Hall, worn smooth by hundreds of thousands of feet over the last century. Stately and elegant, the building was made of gold stone that glittered in sunlight. She was glad to have an opportunity to go inside and look around.

Remi was waiting in the spacious entrance. As usual, Leo was draped over her arm like a spotted handbag. He wagged his tail when he saw her. Once Leo's friend, always Leo's friend.

"Hey, pal," Sasha said, dropping a kiss on one long smooth ear. He was the type of dog you could kiss without asking, and many did. "Are you going to bring me luck today?"

"You might need it," Remi said, frowning. "I had no idea they were *auditioning* for a groomer."

"Auditioning? I thought it was a volunteer gig."

"It is. But so many people volunteered that the City decided to audition. Sorry to spring that on you, Sasha."

"Good thing I came prepared." Sasha held up a black leather bag shaped like a doctor's kit. "You never know when you're going to run into a grooming emergency."

Remi laughed. "That's wonderful! I bet no one else has a kit."

They walked into the meeting room where about 15 people, most of them older women, had gathered around four grooming tables. Four nearly identical goldendoodles stood with their owners, awaiting their makeover. They looked pretty much the same from a distance but Sasha could tell at a glance they weren't. Some were curlier than others, and therefore more likely to be tangled and matted. She whispered a prayer to be assigned the wavy-coated dog at the last station.

A very tall red-headed man called out a greeting and clapped for attention. Everyone turned to face him. "I'm Mike Delaney," he said, "the City's representative for the

Valentine's event. Today we'll start brainstorming our plan for the event, but first we'll audition for head groomer. I'll hand that over to Marsha Wakeman as grooming is a bit out of my bailiwick."

Marsha was at least 60, with dusky skin and slash of white in her otherwise dark hair. She was elegantly dressed in a black suit, which seemed brave for a meeting with at least 10 dogs in the room. Mike himself had a bulldog mutt standing by his side.

"Groomers front and center," Marsha said, clapping.

Sasha kissed Leo again for luck before stepping forward. Marsha directed her to the first grooming station, beside which sat a dog of around 40 pounds. It looked bigger because of the outrageous afro of snarled curls. Sasha's stomach sank. It would be all she could do to get her brush through that mess before the end of the session.

"Excuse me. Marsha." Another groomer—a petite woman with spiky purple hair—was waving from the far end of the row. "This dog is too big for me. I can't even lift it onto the table. I request a trade."

Marsha raised her eyebrows until they disappeared into her white slash of hair, but then she gestured like a traffic cop for Sasha and the other groomer to switch.

Sasha threw Remi a grin as they changed places. Her new model was twice the size of the other, but its wavy coat would be a picnic in comparison. After introducing herself to the owner and then kneeling to meet the dog, she quickly hoisted Feathers onto the table. Then she opened her black bag and pulled out her favorite tools. With a liver treat, she lured Feathers to poke her nose through the grooming noose and then quickly ran her grooming rake through the dog's coat. Two dozen swipes and the big dog was ready for clippers. Ignoring the set provided, she plugged in her own and zipped over the dog with practiced sweeps.

"Excellent home care," she told the owner. "You made my job easy."

Out came the scissors, and the true test began. Anyone could run clippers over a dog, but only someone comfortable with scissors could turn a dog's face into a work of art. The perfection only lasted until the next mud puddle, of course, but a proper groom looked good for at least a month.

After the face and ears, she cut the tail into a perfect sweep, circled the paws, and then snipped the dog's claws. Still in the zone, she used special shears to add texture to the dog's coat and then fluffed until the dog was golden fleece on four paws. As the finishing touch, she pulled out a vial of her own natural oil blend and ran her fingers through the dog's coat. Standing back, she looked at the owner.

"Wow," the owner said. "Wow, wow, wow."

"Hush," Marsha said. "The others are still working."

Indeed, Purple Spikes was still working through her dog's coat with a brush with what sounded like mumbled cursing.

Mike came over to Sasha's grooming station. "You obviously have a good eye," he said, smiling.

Sasha rubbed her forehead with her sleeve. "I see a teddy bear in most non-shedding dogs just waiting to be carved out."

"Interesting," he said, moving on to the other groomers.

Most had barely begun clipping their dogs, and were struggling with the tools provided. The clippers and scissors were dull. "Take mine," Sasha whispered, offering her tools to the woman beside her. She had a regular sharpening routine. It made her feel more confident knowing that she was ready for anything.

Sasha's tools made their way to a third candidate, but Purple Spikes refused them. Instead, she complained loudly that she'd gotten the dud dog of the lot. When the poor pup whimpered under the brush, Marsha called an end to the audition.

Mike took photos of all the dogs, and then let them jump down off the tables. They sat with their owners as Mike explained the committee's role.

"Five weeks goes by in a flash," he said. "And I want you to know that Mayor Bradshaw takes each and every public event very seriously. By next week, I need to present a detailed proposal for our gala itinerary. Let's hear some initial ideas."

"The dog beauty contest is always a winner," Marsha said. "Why mess with success?"

Remi raised her hand. "I love the beauty contest, but maybe we should branch out this year. How about we try a talent show?"

"Too complicated," Marsha said. "Everyone would want special equipment."

"I have to agree. Plus it's outside in February," Mike said. "Always challenging."

Others called out ideas, and were shot down one by one. Finally Sasha raised her hand. When Mike nodded, she said, "Since it's Valentine's Day, maybe we could do something more romantic."

"Everyone loves romance," Remi said. "What were you thinking?"

"How about we take the best of the old and combine it with something new? It's a beauty contest... but for human *and* dog. So the crowd votes on the most attractive man and woman and their dogs. We offer a fancy, intimate dinner as a prize. All the better if romance really sizzles."

"That's a recipe for disaster," Marsha said. "If only single people can enter, we'll hardly get any participants. And the losers will get their feelings hurt."

"I know," Sasha said. "I'd never enter, that's for sure! But everyone loves those survivor-style shows on TV and they love the Thanksgiving rescue pageant. This is just a new spin on that."

Mike gently silenced Marsha's protests and said, "I'll present all ideas to the mayor this week and get his take on it. I've already sent him photos from today's grooming audition, and he got back to me. The lucky winner is... Sasha Wildwood. Welcome aboard. It's wonderful to have fresh faces and ideas as we start a new year in Dorset Hills."

Someone muttered, "Cheat," behind her, and heat jetted up from Sasha's collar. Marsha turned and hissed at Purple Spikes to be quiet.

"Thank you, Mike," Sasha said. "I appreciate this opportunity to contribute to Dorset Hills. What I lack in experience, I make up for with enthusiasm."

"You'll need it," Purple Spikes whispered as she left.

"YOU TOTALLY ROCKED THAT AUDITION," Remi said as they walked along Main Street together.

"Luck favors the prepared groomer," Sasha said, swinging her black bag.

Leo stopped at the Dog Town Tavern for a sprinkle. "I bet you were one of those keeners in high school," Remi said. "I recognize a kindred spirit when I see one."

Sasha laughed. "Guilty. And agreed."

She'd met so many great people lately, but Remi seemed most likely to become a true friend. After a long stretch of feeling adrift in this strange little world, it was nice to feel more anchored. Once the salon was up and running, maybe she could finally start putting down roots.

Standing outside the former Carole's Curls, they looked up at the new sign. "The Model Dog" blazed across it in gold lettering on a deep purple background. To the right of the name the logo featured three fluffy dogs on a runway. Remi's friend Flynn Strathmore, the famous cartoonist, had designed the artwork for the cost of a haircut and some free grooming sessions. Remi had helped her trade services for much of what she needed to transform Carole's Curls into a chic little grooming salon very quickly, since it was a slow time of year. One more weekend with Tiller, Sullivan and their tradesmen pals and all would be ready for the official opening.

It felt like everything was unfolding from some great master plan without Sasha actually knowing how or why. For once, it seemed as if she was in exactly the right place at the right time. That had never happened in her life before.

"Why don't you and Tuni participate in the Valentine's Day event?" Remi said, as Sasha unlocked the door to the shop. "You can be on the committee and still enter."

Sasha raised her knee to fight off Tuni's assault. The dog backed up and bounced a foot ahead of them. "You'd never know I played fetch with her for nearly an hour earlier, would you?"

"Evading the question," Remi said. "I just want to know if you'll spend part of the time on the runway."

Sasha shook her head. "Between Tuni and the shop, I have my hands full."

"Never too full for the right guy," Remi said.

"I thought Bridget was the matchmaker. I've heard

about the happy couples coming out of the Thanksgiving Rescue Pageant."

Remi tossed her coat onto the soon-to-be-retired swivel chair. "You're too fabulous to be single. What gives?"

"What gives is that Lawrence wrecked me for love," Sasha admitted. "I followed his lead without question for three years. Looking back, I have no idea why. It's not like he earned that kind of devotion." She tossed her pink coat on top of Remi's. "Until I learn how to be my own leader, I'm not hooking myself up to anyone else."

"I get that." Remi stepped around Tuni and Leo, who were tumbling in a dappled heap in the small space that would become the waiting room. "I did the same thing, I guess. And by the time Tiller came back to Dorset Hills, I was ready. I just hope it doesn't take you as long as it took me to get my stuff sorted. Ten years."

"It won't. I have good role models," Sasha said, smiling. "I had good friends in Boston, and my sister's amazing, but you guys are already pushing me in ways they never did. How can I help but expand my horizons?"

"You've found your pack," Remi said, laughing.

"I hope so." She laughed too, but she meant it. Her parents had retired to France the previous year and they had never been terribly close. When things had gotten really bad after Lawrence left, she hadn't told anyone—not her friends, not her family. She'd decided to weather it alone. The fact that she'd managed to do so made her proud, but she didn't want to stay a lone wolf forever.

"Do you keep in touch with Lawrence or is it really dead?"

"He's blocked on every channel except one bank account where he could feel free to deposit funds to cover Tuni's vet bills if his conscience ever kicks in." She sat cross-legged on the floor, watching the dogs play. "That was the hardest part: seeing Tuni sick and having no one to help me make decisions. So many tests, so many specialists. And in the end, all they could agree on was that it was a virus."

"What turned things around?"

"Nothing obvious. One day she just started to eat well and gain weight. After that, she never looked back. We're on the right track now, but it cost thousands to learn nothing."

"It's so important to have a great vet," Remi said. "Some of our best are moving out of town."

Snatching Tuni out of the squirming mass of paws and teeth, Sasha hugged her. "She's still the best thing that ever happened to me. Unfortunately, Lawrence was the price of admission."

"Is it too soon to say that it worked out for the best?"

Sasha looked around at the shop and smiled. "Nope. The timing is just about right."

CHAPTER EIGHT

The day of the grand opening was crystal clear and so cold it froze your breath almost before it left your mouth. Sasha had dressed Tuni in a pink faux fur sweater and a matching tutu, mostly because it was cute, but also to keep the dog warm. With the door constantly opening and closing, it was impossible to fend off the chill. She rarely dressed Tuni up because the dog ripped every costume to shreds. But now she was *the* Model Dog, and had to look the part. She'd even polished Tuni's nails pearly pink, since she was offering complimentary peticures to attract clients.

"Oh, Tuni," she said, lifting the dog in her arms. "I'm the worst kind of hypocrite, using you to advertise my wares after making fun of Millie. These things come around and bite me in the butt so fast in Dog Town."

Tuni struggled and squirmed. She wasn't calm and composed like Leo, and never would be, according to Cori. But her training had room for improvement, and Cori had offered to help. If her new friends were right, The Model Dog's future partly hinged on appearances. A beautiful and well-behaved dog would be a definite asset. There was so much riding on this venture that she needed every bit of help and goodwill she could get. Luckily, the salon would provide constant stimulation and socialization for Tuni.

When squirming failed, Tuni tried licking her face.

"No, no. Mommy's got a face full of makeup." She laughed. "Oops, I really am as bad as Griffin Granger says. I never would have imagined being a doting dog mommy two years ago." Tuni thrashed and she set her down. "Fine. You're getting heavy anyway. Someone hasn't been getting enough exercise."

Circling the shop, she couldn't help smiling. The small seating area in the front had a spacious vibe despite the fact that much of the real estate had been reallocated to the private grooming area. Duff's eye for design had really helped. A curved, espresso-colored granite counter offered a sleek, modern focal point, balanced nicely by the antique church pew along one wall. That had been Remi's contribution. The pew had long resided in her basement office at the hospital foundation. She'd moved upstairs now, and her boss Marcus had allowed her to repurpose it.

The rest of the Mafia had provided lots of advice she needed—and some she didn't—but she took it all in stride. She'd never felt more supported in her life, nor so micromanaged. That's what community was all about, she figured.

At two o'clock, she took a deep breath and flipped the sign on the door to "open." It came as no surprise that Remi and Leo were first to arrive. It was a short walk from the mansion that housed the hospital foundation so she visited often. Leo pulled hard to get there and she needed cleats on her boots to stay upright on the perpetually icy sidewalk out front.

The dogs began their usual roughhousing the second he was through the door.

"Leo, we have to be on our best behavior today," Remi said.

Sasha hugged her and they ended up jumping up and down. "Can you believe it?" she asked. "This is the best day of my life, Remi. Rivalled only by the day I got Tuni. Thank you so much for all your help."

"Are you kidding? I've loved every minute of it. And once you start pulling rare dogs in here for grooming, you won't be able to keep me away."

Remi had an encyclopedic knowledge of dog breeds and a collector's eye. She kept an online scrapbook of photos of exotic dogs living in Dorset Hills, and competed with her friend and colleague Arden Lee in a game they called "Dogspotting."

"I'm hoping to build from the basics," Sasha said. "Doodles and wheatens and schnauzers. I wouldn't have a clue how to groom a pumi or a barbet."

Remi shrugged. "That's what the Internet's for, right?"

The door bells chimed and the Rescue Mafia came in—Bridget and Beau, Duff, Cori and Maisie, the tall groomer with blonde corkscrew curls. Nika was working that afternoon and couldn't attend.

Duff had recommended they not attend at all, lest it raise concerns about connections with the Rescue Mafia, but Sasha had insisted. This opening wouldn't be grand at all without them, and she wasn't convinced their rep was as bad as they said. In fact, she suspected Cori liked to inflate it.

Duff and Maisie kept the coffee fresh and set out treats from Chez Poodelle, the only French bakery in town. The sugar cookies were beautifully and cleverly decorated with various dog breeds.

Soon the small space was so tightly packed it was hard to mix and mingle. Sasha lost track of Tuni, but Cori had appointed herself canine ringleader, for which everyone was grateful. Dogs from the neighborhood were coming in and they could have gotten testy in such close confines, but a few sharp barks from Cori put everything right.

Sasha was standing close to the door when a dark-haired woman came in carrying a mid-sized red doodle hybrid. "George!" The cry rippled through the crowd and Mim Gardiner smiled. Hands shot out to pat him and he accepted them calmly.

"We've been working with Cori," Mim said to no one in particular. "George had to learn some manners."

Cori ducked under arms and swooped in to collect George. She set him promptly on the floor and let him navigate the sea of boots. "He has paws for a reason, Mim. If you carry him around all the time he'll get a Napoleon complex."

"I just don't want to lose him again," Mim said, making a futile grab for the leash.

"That's the attitude that gets you demoted down your pack until you're the one following George's lead," Cori said, before disappearing into the crowd.

Mim turned back to Sasha and rolled her eyes. "Well, I've been told. But with my hands free, I can give you a hug and congratulate you properly.

"It's good to see you again," Sasha said. "Thank you so much for coming."

The hug lasted longer than most—so long, in fact, that Remi paused with her coffee cup in midair to stare.

"How are you doing?" Mim whispered.

"Good. Good. I'm really good." Sasha's words were brisk and brittle.

Pulling back, Mim raised her eyebrows. "That was about two goods too many."

"No really, I'm fine. Perfectly healthy."

"Which is why you skipped your last appointment at the clinic," Mim said. "The one where we normally talk about... things."

"I know I should have come, but I'd started the grooming course." She gave a broad sweep with her arm. "Anyway, you can see how well everything's going, Mim."

"I can, and I'm happy for you. Just remember that my door's always open. At the clinic and beyond, okay?"

Remi swooped over with a cup of coffee for Mim and Sasha faded into the crowd. Mim wouldn't say a word about how they'd met. She was the consummate professional—the type of nurse you could spill your darkest secrets to... and Sasha had. But those dark days had passed and she wanted to focus on bright skies ahead.

A blast of cold air hit her as the door opened and stayed open. Bartholomew Barnes and Puck were trying to get into the shop but the crowd was nearly impenetrable.

"Incoming," Sasha called, rushing to Bart's aid. She cleared a path so that he could get to the counter.

"I don't need your help, young lady," he said. "That's what canes are for."

He gave a woman a little jab between her shoulder blades and she moved away from the cookie tray quickly. Bart leaned over and made a long, considered decision before selecting a bright-eyed husky cookie.

"Care to explain your choice?" Sasha asked. "I would have pegged you for the spaniel."

He took a bite and crumbs dropped onto the floor, to be

snuffled up by Puck. "You read too much into everything. This one has the most frosting, that's all."

Sasha pressed a small card into his hand. "This is for a free peticure for Puck. But you know I'd be thrilled to give him a full groom."

"Meddling." Bart declined the card, but accepted the steaming mug Duff offered him, along with one of her blazing smiles. "Now there's a gracious lady. All smiles and no direction on how to stir my coffee."

"This is a grooming salon, Bart. Advice comes with the territory."

He finished his cookie before saying, "Puck and I are happy as we are. We're not like the moneybag clients you'll need to court."

"That's not how I operate, Bart. I put the dogs first and always will."

Leaning over the tray, he selected a cookie featuring an adorable Pomeranian. After admiring it for a second, he smashed it with a spoon. Sasha winced. "There. See?" he said. "You're upset over a broken cookie. You'll need to toughen up, my young friend. Business in this town isn't for the fainthearted. It's not all sugar cookies and lavender oil." He raised his nose and sniffed. "You're piping that in here, aren't you?"

"It's calming for dogs and humans," Sasha said. "Except irascible men, it seems."

He let his glasses slide down his nose and stared at her with eyes that were still sharp. "Insult me *after* you get your ribbon-cutting gift." He reached into his worn coat and pulled out a large plush dog. "Every shop needs a mascot."

Sasha turned it in her hands. "It's a Welshie! How did you find it?"

"The tag said springer spaniel. I figured that was close

enough." He held up a hand to fend off Sasha's hug. "Oh no you don't. The coffee and sweets are thanks enough. I wish you well, young lady, but I suggest you keep your eyes wide open. Hear me?"

"Eyes wide open," she repeated. "But what do I need to be worried about?"

"Don't worry at all. Just work hard and pay attention."

She pushed through the crowd to the glass shelves near the counter and stood on tiptoe to set the stuffed dog on the very top looking out. It felt like a talisman that would keep the shop safe from whatever threat Bart anticipated.

When she turned back, he was gone. For an old man, he could really fly when he felt like it.

"WHEW!" Remi collapsed onto the long oak pew running along one side of the shop. It fit perfectly and added the touch of quaint charm every Dog Town establishment needed. "That was some turnout. You must have given out fifty cards for free peticures."

"More," Sasha said. "I'll be working for free for months to come."

"Great business strategy," Cori said, from the floor, where she sat cross-legged, surrounded by dogs. None of them actually sat on her lap. They respected her too much to take the liberty. But they couldn't resist hanging around, even Beau. George and Leo lolled nearby and Tuni flipped on her back. Her faux fur sweater was bedraggled and askew, and the tutu had been neatly snipped off by Leo's sharp incisors.

Leaning over, Cori stared at Tuni. "What the—?"

"What's wrong?" Sasha asked, instantly alert.

Cori held up one hand. "Sasha, stay. Bridget, come."

Both women obeyed the trainer's commands. Bridget knelt beside Cori and examined Tuni. Her eyes widened, and she ran an exploratory hand over Tuni's belly. The dog didn't move a muscle. She was blissfully exhausted by the festivities.

Bridget sat back on her heels and shared a wordless exchange with Cori. Finally she turned perplexed eyes on Sasha. "I think you might have a little problem. It's not the end of the world, but definitely a little problem."

"Is she okay?" Sasha dropped to her knees and crawled over. The dog looked well, and was finally filling out nicely.

"What's going on?" Remi asked. "Can you two drop the mind-meld and fill the rest of us in?"

"Maybe we should talk about it later," Bridget said. "When everyone's—"

Cori raised a hand to interrupt. "Tuni's pregnant," she said. "There's no good way to say it, and no point pussy-footing around."

"Pregnant!" Sasha braced herself on the heels of her hands and stared at Cori. "What do you mean?"

"I mean knocked up. With pup. Buns in the oven."

"Don't joke, Cori," Bridget said. "This is serious."

Mim jumped to her feet and pressed Sasha's shoulders till she settled backwards on her butt. "You're white as a ghost. Take some deep breaths or you'll faint."

"Tuni can't be pregnant," Sasha whispered. "She's getting spayed next week."

"Locked barn, horse gone," Cori said.

"Stop it," Duff said. "It's not funny."

Cori wasn't smiling. "I would never laugh over unwanted pups."

"Then don't be a smartass." Duff rested a gentle hand on Sasha's shoulder. "Do you think it's possible?"

"It's not only possible, but probable," Cori said. She was like a popcorn popper, always firing out that last volley when you think it's all done.

"But she's never unsupervised," Sasha said. "Never out alone."

"Maybe she's just in heat," Remi said. "Did she have a heat?"

"Not that I know of. I've seen nothing different about her. Nothing at all." She stared down at her dog, and somehow the signs were suddenly obvious. "She felt a bit heavier than usual. I thought she was finally filling out."

"Maybe we're jumping the gun here," Bridget said.

"We're not," Cori interjected.

"We're not veterinarians, you mean," Bridget said. "And this is a vet's call. Rather than get more fussed, why don't we head over now and let an expert confirm or deny."

Duff helped Sasha to her feet, saying, "Remi, Maisie and I will stay here and get the place cleaned up so you don't come back to a mess."

"I'm going with her," Remi said. "She'll need Leo."

"She has her own dog," Cori said.

"Leo's a professional therapy dog," Remi said, hooking him up. "We'll pitch in when we get back. Hopefully, it'll be a false alarm."

"I'll stay," Mim said. Her brow was creased with worry. "But take good care of her, won't you?"

Cori gave her a withering look. "I always take good care of dogs."

Mim withered her back. "I meant Sasha. I always take good care of humans, remember?"

"I'll be fine," Sasha said. "This can't be true. I don't believe it."

Cori's mouth opened, but Bridget spoke first. "There's a time for speculation and a time for expert opinion," she said. "Everybody into the van. Now."

CHAPTER NINE

The long drive to the vet was strangely quiet. Sasha was relieved no one bothered with small talk when there was nothing good to be said. Even Remi, who usually filled awkward silences, kept her lips sealed and her hands busy patting Leo. When he would stay on her lap, that is. He kept trying to worm his way over to Sasha's. The dog had an unerring instinct for knowing who needed him most. But Sasha had Tuni wrapped in a hug and she wasn't letting her go. Normally Tuni wouldn't sit still for that, but she was simply too tired to resist.

"Why go so far?" Sasha asked, at last. The highest hills were behind them now, and they were twisting down toward the town of Milverton. "We passed a dozen vets already."

"We like this guy," Bridget said, keeping her eyes on the road as she drove. It was nearly dark already. "He gives us a good deal."

"Plus he keeps his mouth shut," Cori said. "He's got a good head on his shoulders, unlike the vets in Dorset Hills."

"There are good vets in town," Bridget said. "Nika works for one."

"They've got a grapevine," Cori said. "Sooner or later things leak."

Bridget nodded. "We wouldn't want something like this to get around."

"The less said the better in Dog Town," Cori said. "The old guard is full of vipers."

"I'm old guard and I don't sting," Remi said. "The new guard is even more judgemental if you ask me."

Cori shoulders twitched, as if she wanted to argue, but she let it go. "Everyone judges everyone, I guess. Even me."

"Especially you," Bridget said, but there was a smile in her voice.

"Because I can. I even have good hair now." Cori glanced behind. "Thanks to you."

Sasha's throat tightened. If Cori was trying to cheer her up, the situation must be dire indeed. Her mind raced with possible scenarios, each more frightening than the last. She was clutching Tuni so tight the dog's breathing was labored.

"It's okay, we're here," Remi said, as they turned into a parking lot outside a low, grey brick building. "Dr. Benson will get things sorted out."

"We'll wait in the van if you don't mind," Bridget said. "We're here so often, and we don't want Dr. Benson to get blowback for helping us."

"I've got it," Sasha said. "It's my problem, and you've done enough."

"I'm coming in," Remi said. "Leo loves Dr. Benson."

The dogs walked up the stairs ahead of them and Sasha opened the door. Remi passed through it first and then paused. "Hello there," she said.

Sasha could barely rein in her panic long enough to look

around the waiting room. When she did, she saw Griffin Granger sitting at the far end with Grover on the seat beside him. The bulldog was really too big for the seat, or at least the wrong proportions; one hind leg hung down awkwardly.

"Oh," Sasha said. "It's you."

Grover struggled to coordinate his limbs, but he was afraid to jump down. Griffin grabbed him, one hand looped through his collar, the other around the dog's barrel chest. "Grover, stay."

Sasha raised her hand, palm up. "Stay, Grover. We'll say hi later, okay?"

The assistant ushered Sasha right into an examination room, and it gave her a spark of satisfaction to see Griffin's indignation that she was served first. It was good to have friends in low places.

Dr. Benson didn't waste a second. "On the table," he said. Sasha didn't bend immediately over, so he picked up Tuni himself. When the dog licked his face, he smiled. He was attractive, in a never-see-the-sun-totally-committed-to-animals kind of way. His skin and hair were fair, and his eyes so light they were barely blue. "You think she's pregnant?" he asked.

"She can't be," Sasha said. "She's never unsupervised and my yard's fenced."

"She wouldn't be the first to go over or under a fence," he said. "A dog in heat can move mountains."

"But she wasn't in heat," Sasha said. "There would have been blood, right? And she was at my vet's just over a month ago. Surely they'd have noticed something."

The vet examined Tuni quickly. She didn't resist when he palpated her abdomen.

After that, he set the dog on the floor and leaned against the counter with his arms crossed. "Sometimes a first heat is silent and there's really no sign. It doesn't mean the dog can't get pregnant, unfortunately."

Sasha's hands clenched around the leash and she brought them up to her chin in a gesture of prayer. "No."

"I'm afraid so. She looks about four weeks gone."

"A dog's gestation is sixty-three days, correct?" Remi said.

"Correct," he said, stooping to pat Leo at last. "Give or take."

"And what are Sasha's options?" Remi said. "At this point."

Standing, the vet blinked at her a few times. "I don't like to do pregnant spays, if that's what you're asking. No judgment. It's just risky for the dog, especially halfway through."

"We're not quite halfway, though," Remi said. "There's still a day or two left. Surely there's some allowance when the dog is so young. Are you saying you never do?"

Dr. Benson shook his head. "I prefer not to, but I see this isn't an ideal situation. I assume you have no idea who the sire is?"

Sasha shook her head and repeated. "She's never been out of the yard."

"Well, Tuni must have found herself a boyfriend somewhere."

"What if it was a huge dog?" Remi asked. "Like a mastiff or a Great Pyrenees?"

"The odds are against it," the vet said. "The mechanics would be awkward."

Sasha flinched at the thought. "Oh my goodness."

"You're anthropomorphizing," he said. "As much as we love our pets, they really are just animals following their instincts. Tuni would have said 'hell yes,' to the stud in question."

Still cringing, Sasha said, "It could be a pit bull. Or anything, really."

"Pit bulls are banned in Dorset Hills, of course. In fact, with the city's new neuter policy coming into effect, I'm surprised she found an intact dog in the timeframe she had."

"She didn't leave her yard. The... uh... stud must have gotten in somehow."

"Check your neighborhood to see who's avoided neutering despite recent pressure from the City. There will always be some. Then we'll have a better idea what we're dealing with."

"I couldn't wait to neuter Leo," Remi said. "The second he started humping... snip-snip."

"With large breeds, people often wait till the dog is a year to castrate. I don't disagree with that approach, as long as they can handle any behavioral issues. I believe in personal accountability." He crossed his arms and smiled. "Dorset Hills Council doesn't always see eye to eye with me. That's why I moved my practice out of town two years ago."

"Personal accountability," Sasha said. "This is *my* fault. No matter how it happened."

"No blame and no judgement," he said. "Things happen with dogs. They're animals."

He offered her the box of tissues and she grabbed a handful. She hadn't realized she was crying. "Tuni was scheduled to be spayed this week. She missed her first two appointments because she was sick."

"It'll be okay," he said. "Dogs have pups all the time without any trouble. Raising them will be a pain in the neck, but it won't be hard to find homes for them. It's dog country."

"But she's so young. What if there are 10 of them? Or what if they're huge, like..." She groped around for a breed. "Like English bulldogs."

"We could give her an ultrasound or X-ray to make sure everything looks normal. It's easier to see what's going on later in the pregnancy."

"Or you could have her spayed," Remi reminded her.

"He's said that's risky, too." The tears were coming faster than she could mop them up. She took the entire box of tissues from the vet's hand. "I've spent months worrying about her health and she was finally okay. I just want her to be well."

The vet patted her shoulder awkwardly. "This will end up okay. Remember, dogs have pups all the time." Turning back to his laptop, he tapped out some notes. "I'll do some bloodwork on Tuni. You can go out to the desk and leave your contact information. I'll send you some notes so you can make an informed decision."

Sasha followed Remi out and offered her credit card to the clerk at the desk.

"It'll be okay," Remi whispered. "You heard the vet."

Nodding, Sasha turned just in time to sidestep a thundering bowling ball on four paws. Grover hit the desk, bounced back and turned. This time he stuck his head between her knees from behind. She looked down to see him looking up, his tongue lolling to one side as his scrunched face offered a wide grin. Despite everything that had happened, Sasha couldn't help grinning back. "Grovey," she said. "How's my buddy?"

"No baby talk," Griffin said, joining them. "I don't want him getting used to that nonsense."

"You mean you don't want him to be happy?" Remi asked. "Because he looks happy to me."

Sasha kept her head down, but that only meant tears dropped directly onto Grover's face. He blinked as one hit him in the eye and licked another off his nose. Two more splashed onto the tile floor.

"What are you doing— Oh." Griffin bit off whatever he was going to say. "I'm sorry. Is Tuni all right?"

"Fine. She's fine. Everything is fine." More tears rained down on Grover, and rather than back away, the dog just wriggled harder, as if to cheer her up. "You're a good boy, Grovey. You're the bestie-westie."

This time Griffin didn't complain.

A veterinary assistant brought Tuni out, and she greeted Grover with her usual gusto.

"We'd better get going, Sash," Remi said. "Let's get back to the salon, okay?"

"I thought you got fired," Griffin said, crouching to hold Grover back. "Or downsized. Laid off."

"Promoted, more like," Remi said. "She's got her own shop now. The Model Dog on Main Street. The grand opening was today."

"Congratulations," Griffin said, and he sounded as if he meant it. "Glad things worked out."

"Thanks," Sasha said, bending right over to kiss Grover on the head. "Bye, buddy. Whatever you're here for, I hope it goes well."

"He has the sniffles, that's all," Griffin said.

"Respiratory problems are endemic to the breed," Remi said. "As are skin conditions, cardiac problems, cherry eye, and hip dysplasia. They drown easily, too."

"Remi!" Sasha looked up quickly. "Don't scare him."

"I'm sure Griffin knows the risks," Remi said.

"I meant Grover," Sasha said. "I guess I'm scared *for* him after hearing that."

"He's fine. Everything is fine," Griffin said, echoing her earlier words.

She wiped her face with her sleeve and lifted her foot to free Grover. "I hope you're fine, buddy. But we've gotta get going now."

"Look, I'm sorry about whatever happened in there," Griffin said.

"Thanks," she said, forcing a smile. "We're good."

He was still on his knee beside Grover. "Okay, because I wanted to tell you something you probably don't want to hear."

"Let's pass on that for today," Remi said, pulling on Sasha's sleeve. "Thanks for the warning."

"Wait." He struggled to restrain Grover. "I think you'll—"

"Nice seeing you, Grover," Sasha said, as Remi towed her out. "Keep smiling."

CHAPTER TEN

The next morning was bleak in the way only Dorset Hills in January could be. Low dark clouds threatened snow but didn't deliver their bright cargo. A cutting wind blew drifts along the streets like ghosts. Meanwhile, the shops on Main Street had started turning off Christmas lights and dismantling pretty displays. It was the first time Sasha had experienced the unique Dog Town post-holiday slump. Where there was an excessive high, a low surely followed. All the excitement of auditioning for the Valentine's show and opening the salon had merely delayed it.

She turned the key in the lock, wondering how she'd get through the day. "It's okay, Tuni," she said. The dog seemed curious about Sasha's mood but not worried. From puppyhood she'd always been upbeat. That party spirit was one of her big selling points, but it had ultimately led to her undoing.

The door bells chimed as she was hanging up her coat in the back room.

"Coffee?" Remi called out.

"You're a lifesaver." Sasha came to the front of the shop.

Remi's smile was so infectious that her face twitched in response. *Turn that frown upside down*, her mom had always said. Now it was pretty much ingrained, no matter how grim the circumstances.

"Even better," Remi said, rustling a paper bag out of her purse. "Croissants from Chez Poodelle. Still warm."

"I wish I could, but my stomach's queasy."

"Sympathetic morning sickness?" Remi asked.

Sasha's stomach clenched and sent up a little geyser of acid. "Sounds about right."

Remi's smile faded. "Sorry. I know I shouldn't joke."

"It's okay. I can still see the humor. My dog is eating for 10. This morning, she got a box of cereal off the counter, something she's never done before. I didn't know she was capable of doing that." She looked down at the dog, whose tail beat steadily as she pranced around Leo. "I didn't know she was capable of a lot of things, obviously."

"Any insights on how it happened?" Remi asked. She took off her coat and threw it onto the old oak pew.

Leaning on the cold, curved counter, Sasha nodded. "I found out the *how* and the *when*. The only thing missing is the 'who.'"

"Tell me everything." Remi settled into the pew and crossed her arms. "Marcus thinks I'm at a meeting, by the way. I'm good for a couple of hours."

Sasha walked over to the door and locked it again. She turned the sign to "closed" and sat down beside Remi. "Well, after I got home last night, I had a shot of whiskey for courage. Then I went outside with a flashlight and rooted around behind the scrub cedars and the old shed at the back of the yard. That's where I found a hole under the fence. More accurately, I found the remains of a hole. It had been filled in recently—before the ground froze."

"Filled in? Tuni is smart enough to cover her tracks?"

"Only if she's also smart enough to use a hammer and put up a new board across the bottom." She stared down at the dog, who was nipping Leo's back paws to get him to play. "She's smart but not that smart. So I figured it was more likely the handiwork of my landlord."

"Did you confront him?"

"I did. After another shot of whisky, I went upstairs and got the whole story. On the weekend I did my grooming certification in mid-December, he let her out twice. The second time she disappeared for about fifteen minutes, he said."

"Longer, I'm sure," Remi said. "First she had to find the stud and then the mating process itself can take up to half an hour. What happens is—"

She held up her hand. "No thanks. Queasy, remember?" Remi's encyclopedic knowledge of dogs extended well past rare breeds. Why she'd gone into fundraising instead of a veterinary field was a mystery.

"But it's totally fascinating if you just get past—"

"Not going to happen. I don't need to know more than the bare facts. Specifically, Tuni got out, got herself knocked up, and came home. Mr. Morrison thought no harm had been done and repaired the hole in the fence."

Getting up, Remi paced across the small seating area. "Did you tell him she's pregnant?"

Sasha shook her head. "As Cori would say, it's on a need-to-know basis. And he doesn't need to know."

"Good. The fewer people who do, the better." Remi perched again and waited for Sasha to speak. When she didn't, she finally asked, "Have you decided?"

Toying with the lid of her coffee cup, Sasha nodded. "I can't do the spay." Her eyes filled with tears again. They were puffy and red from crying most of the night as it was. "I know you think I should, but I just can't."

"It's not that I think you *should*," Remi said. "I don't like the idea of it either. I just think it would be easier."

"On Tuni or me?"

"Both. At least, I think so. From my research, it doesn't look like a terribly high risk surgery with a good vet. At this stage the puppies aren't—"

Sasha raised her hand. "I don't want to picture it."

"Well, let's focus on you, then. You've just opened the doors here. How will you handle a litter of pups next month? They're due right around Valentine's day."

"I'd better quit the planning committee. I don't want to make promises I can't see through."

Remi patted her arm. "I've got a better idea. And I talked to the Mafia about it last night, because I figured you'd tip this way."

Sasha raised her eyes from the coffee cup. "What's your idea?"

"Cori knows someone. She always knows someone. There's a retired dog breeder down near Milverton. She could take Tuni for the last week or two of the pregnancy and look after them all until the puppies wean."

"Like a home for wayward dogs?" Sasha asked.

"Exactly. Tuni will disappear in a few weeks and you'll tell everyone she's going to training boot camp. People totally support that sort of thing here."

"I can't send Tuni away for that long. She's my dog, and it's my responsibility."

"It'll pass faster than you think. You'll use the time to build the business and make a name for yourself in the community. That'll be good for both of you."

Sasha got up and walked to the door. She had to step

around Tuni and Leo. They were kibitzing as if nothing had changed, when *everything* had changed. "I don't think so. I need to figure out a way to manage at home. I can't believe I let this happen."

Remi got up, too, and stood beside her, staring out onto Main Street. It was starting to fill with people and dogs, despite the cold. Even in January, the dogs had to get out and Main Street had everything most people needed. "Okay. I'm going to stop beating around the bush here. I like to be tactful, but you're new to Dog Town and you don't know our ways. So I need to be blunt. May I?" She gulped her own coffee and waited for permission.

"Okay. I'm ready for it."

"I'm not, though," Remi muttered. "I hate this." She set her coffee cup on the ledge by the door, and scooped up Leo with her right arm. He went from playful to docile in an instant. The dog knew his job inside out. "Here's the thing, Sasha. If word gets out that Tuni is pregnant, it will hurt your business. People will say you're not careful with your dog and may not be with theirs." Sasha started to protest but Remi raised a hand and forged on. "It's not right and it's not fair. It just is. There's a good side of Dog Town and a bad side. You want to stay on the good side, right?"

"I—I have to. I dumped all my savings in this place. And if you're right—"

"I'm right, unfortunately. I've lived here all my life. Things have changed, and the judgement is real."

"Then it wouldn't stop at losing the shop. No grooming salon would hire me if this news got out. My training would be wasted. More money down the drain. I'd either have to leave Dorset Hills and start fresh somewhere else, or try working as a hairstylist again."

Stroking Leo, Remi sighed. "Even then you could have trouble. This place has a long memory."

Sasha turned from the door and started pacing. Tuni paced with her happily, tail aloft. "So you're saying my career is going to be destroyed because of an accidental pregnancy?"

"Not necessarily. I'm saying it's possible that your reputation could take a hit if the news got out. But if you'd just—"

She threw Remi a fierce stare. "Aborting isn't an option."

"I know that. But fostering her out for the delivery could work beautifully."

"But it'll still show, right? Before and after. Will she ever... regain her girlish figure?"

"Not fully, but she has all those feathers. Grow them out. The bushier the better. If anyone asks, you blame sagginess on a spay. It happens."

"She is pretty bushy under there. It's the upside of the Welshie over other spaniels."

"Not only that, you're in the perfect position to dress her up."

"True." Sasha lifted her head, finally seeing a pinpoint of light at the end of the tunnel. "Sweaters. Dresses. Snazzy little vests. All the things I used to make fun of, especially for sporting dogs."

"The frillier the better. You have the perfect excuse as the owner of The Model Dog."

Kneeling down, Sasha tipped Tuni's chin up. "If you can't be a model dog... be a dog model."

Now Remi laughed. "There you go. Sasha's back."

Sasha sat cross-legged and Tuni climbed into her lap, turned twice and settled. Running her hand over the dog's sleek head and back, she said, "I felt like I'd lost my little girl."

"I know, but the vet was right about anthropomorphizing. They're just animals." She cuddled Leo under her chin and grinned. "Except Leo."

There was a knock at the door, and Sasha got up to unlock it. Her first official customers had arrived.

CHAPTER ELEVEN

Two smiling, grey-haired women walked in with their dogs.

"Can we redeem our peticures?" one asked.

"Absolutely. Welcome!"

Remi grabbed Tuni's collar and led her into the back room. Before the ladies had even taken off their coats, Tuni was back, wearing a faux shearling coat. One woman owned a bichon and the other a miniature poodle. There was much milling about as the dogs made their acquaintance.

Sasha put on her game face and grabbed her peticure kit, which contained two dozen colors of nail polish. The women oohed and aahed" as they made their selections. Meanwhile, she sat on the floor, letting the dogs get used to her. Within a few moments, the bichon was happily ensconced in her lap and she could start snipping. When she could avoid the formality of the grooming table, she often did. It made for more comfortable canine clients.

Remi got the conversation going and all lamented the winter doldrums that had descended on the town.

"Valentine's Day will be with us before you know it,"

she said. "Sasha and I are on the planning committee and we're going to show you a good time. We're just waiting for the mayor to approve our proposal."

Gladys, the older of the women, sniffed. "Bill Bradshaw is so full of himself. He's gone too far with that dog court. I feel terrible for Marti Forrester. I get the feeling it won't end well for her."

"Knee-jerk policy making," said Ruby, the other customer. "After the court hearing about the humping dog, the City's introducing regulations about castrating and spaying. We should be able to make decisions about whether to neuter our dogs."

Gladys said, "I don't think it's such a bad idea that males dogs be neutered, actually."

Sasha kept her eyes on the bichon in her lap, who was happily submitting to mauve polish.

"You think all owners should have to neuter by City policy?" Ruby argued. "Why invite Bill Bradshaw into our living rooms? We're all mature enough to make the right decisions about our dogs."

"Some people aren't, though," Gladys said. "Isn't that always the problem? I can name a handful of male dogs right now who'd be better off snipped. Obviously people spay their girls, so the humping is more an issue of dominance than anything. There's a boxer on Cosburn Avenue who humps anything with a heartbeat, including the postman. And there's a Rhodesian Ridgeback on Oakdene Drive that's just as bad, only bigger. When you have a delicate dog like my Stella, seeing these big bruisers coming at you is terrifying. They've knocked her over a few times. What if I'm next? I have half a mind to report them to the Tattletail Hotline."

Sasha stifled a nervous giggle and turned it into a cough.

"Are you all right, dear?" Ruby said. "You could catch a chill sitting the floor like that."

"All good," Sasha said, releasing the bichon and reaching out to catch the mini poodle. "I'm surprised to hear there are so many unneutered male dogs around. I wouldn't think people would want to deal with that."

Remi threw her a warning glance and she got to work on the poodle.

"Well, it's male owners of course," Gladys said. "They feel it reflects on their masculinity. Usually it's the big macho dogs that still have their parts. Like that brindle bulldog on Browning Street. The owner looks like some kind of extremist, with his shaved head and tattoos. Of course he'd want an intact dog."

"Grover?" Sasha said. "I met him at my old salon. He's actually a sweetheart. I have to admit I didn't really notice."

"Well, I suppose you had enough to handle with Mildred Trowbridge." Ruby looked at Gladys and they rolled their eyes in unison. "Some people spend so much time with dogs that they end up half dog themselves."

Sasha willed herself not to laugh. "I'm so grateful she gave me my start in grooming. I really needed those practicum hours to get my certification. Otherwise I'd never have been able to jump on this location."

"Poor Carole." The women's voices overlapped.

"She's starting to get up and around now," Ruby said. "I stopped coming here years ago, though. Her cuts were so dated. Her answer to every hair challenge was a perm. Who perms anymore?"

"Hopefully she can find something else to do when she's ready," Gladys said. "It's not like she had money to spare. Not after her husband left her for the dog walker."

"No!" Sasha said, looking up from the poodle's toes. "That's terrible."

"Happens more often than you'd think," Ruby said. "It's cliché in Dog Town. Like the nanny everywhere else."

"You definitely want to hire an ugly walker," Gladys agreed. "Better yet, a male. No temptation at all."

"Except to the lady of the house," Ruby said. "That happens plenty, too."

Sasha's hands shook from holding back nervous laughter. Leo struggled to get down from Remi's lap and draped himself at Sasha's side, since her lap was full. Just his warm body was enough to calm her down. Remi did her part by lobbing conversational topics to the women like chum to sharks. Finally she said, "So we have a new bronze. I was surprised to see the corgi outside the Carlaw movie complex."

"I'm sure the queen would disapprove," Ruby said. "I think the proportions are a little off. The fiberglass corgi that disappeared from the Barkingham Palace café was a closer likeness."

And so it went as Sasha sped through the poodle's claws, then got up off the floor. The women cooed delightedly over their dogs' pretty toes, but she had the feeling they'd stab her in the back as the door closed behind them.

"We'll be sure to stop by soon," Ruby said. "You've done a marvelous job, and the place is lovely."

"It seems like a new groomer pops up every week lately," Gladys said. "The complimentary nail trims are a big help for those of us on a limited budget."

"So glad I could help," Sasha said, realizing her free offer wasn't necessarily going to generate the traffic she'd expected.

"I'd love to bring Stella here for a cut," Ruby said. "But

I'm loyal to my regular groomer. We're like that in Dog Town. Loyal to the core."

"I hope you'll be able to drum up enough business, Sasha," Gladys said. "Because you seem like a lovely girl. And Tuni is just adorable. If you like sporting dogs."

Their goodbyes cut off abruptly as Sasha shut the door and leaned against it.

CHAPTER TWELVE

"I need to take a shower in the dog tub. I feel dirty after that conversation."

"Told you," Remi said. "That's our old guard. And the new guard just judges in a different way. You'll see."

"Can I talk you into getting me another coffee?" Sasha said. "Make it a double."

Remi got her coat and took Leo with her down the street to Puccini Café.

While she was gone, there was a kerfuffle at the door, and a rattle against the glass. Sasha turned to see a woman in her twenties, standing behind a wheelchair. In the older woman's lap sat a perky Yorkie cross.

Opening the door, Sasha said, "Hello! And welcome to The Model Dog."

The older woman's eyes darted around, taking everything in. "Oh my. Everything's changed. Everything."

"This is my grandmother," the young woman said. "Carole, the previous proprietor. I'm her granddaughter, Melanie."

"Oh my goodness," Sasha said, standing back so they could roll by. "Carole, it's an honor to meet you. I've heard a lot about you."

"I saw Ruby and Gladys leaving, so I'm sure it was all sugar and spice," Carole said. "They weren't my biggest fans, I'm afraid."

"They were very sorry about your accident," Sasha said. "Everyone is. I have to admit I feel terrible taking over the space under the circumstances."

"It's not your fault. It's his," Carole said. Her warm brown eyes crinkled at the corners as she patted her dog. "I tripped over this little treasure and at my age sometimes it all goes down like a house of cards."

"Grandma, you're going to be fine." Melanie patted Carole's shoulder.

"It could happen to anyone," Sasha said. "I trip over Tuni all the time. She likes to keep me on my toes."

"That's a sweet little sweater," Carole said. "I can't get Caesar to wear one, even on a cold day like this. He's too proud."

"He'd prefer to sit on your lap and soak up your body heat," Melanie said.

"Would you like me to trim his claws while you're here?" Sasha asked.

"You can try," Carole said. "He's spunky."

"He's an ass," Melanie said. "Watch your fingers."

"Let me take him to the back then. Usually they're better when they're out of their owners' sight."

Caesar took a lunge at her hand when she reached for the leash Carole offered. "Oh, I'm so sorry, dear. Caesar, you bad boy."

Sasha had learned in grooming school not to show that

aggressive displays fazed her. She put on a bright smile and said, "Let's go, you little character. We'll get you all trimmed up."

The dog put on his brakes, refusing to follow. "Just pick him up," Carole said.

"I wouldn't if I were you," Melanie said. "I'd apply my boot to the situation."

Sasha laughed. "I won't last long if I start kicking my clients." Instead she did the next best thing by pulling a liver treat out of her pocket. Caesar's ears came forward and he picked up his feet like a thoroughbred horse. "There we go. You can be bought, like most of us."

In the grooming room, it took a steady drip of liver bits to get Caesar to comply with his trim. His beady eyes seemed to measure each crumb to see if it was worthy currency, and as a result it took about 15 minutes for a three-minute job.

By the time she let him pull her back out, Remi was talking to Carole like an old friend. "My mom still swears by your perms," she said.

"It's a magic cure for some women," Carole said. "There's a time and a place for them, no matter how out of vogue they go."

"You'll be back on perm patrol before you know it," Melanie said.

Carole's smile faded. "I'm not sure I'll ever be able to stand that long, let alone do the shampooing and such. Hairstyling is a job for the young."

"It's hard physical labor, I can attest to that," Sasha said. "I had back and shoulder problems after 10 years as a stylist. Changing over to dogs isn't necessarily easier, but at least it uses different muscles."

"I wish you well, my dear," Carole said, as Melanie turned the chair. "This place is full of happy memories and I like to think they infuse a place."

"I do too," Sasha said. "I can't tell you how glad I am to be here. I'm just so sorry about why you left."

"Everything happens for a reason," Carole said. "And I'm going to get to the bottom of what Caesar taught me by nearly killing me."

"I can't wait to hear this story," Mel said. "Caesar's mythology expands every day."

"I don't know where I'd be without the little rascal. I probably wouldn't have bothered recovering if it weren't for him."

"You wouldn't need to recover if it weren't for him," Mel said.

"Always so cynical," Carole said. "I prefer to see the glass as half full."

"Me too," Sasha said. "We have a lot in common, Carole."

The warm brown eyes looked back at her, and twinkled. "That we do. I think we're going to be good friends when I get back on my pins."

"Caesar won't like having to use his own feet again," Mel said.

"Oh Mel, it's almost like you don't like Caesar sometimes."

"Who wouldn't like Caesar?" Sasha said.

"That's so sweet, dear. I really didn't think you'd pull it off. Even the vet hates trimming Caesar's claws. You certainly have a way about you."

Sasha waited till Carole was out of sight before turning to Remi. "Geez. She let me do that knowing I might lose my hand. I've learned about Dog Town today and it's not even noon."

Remi nodded as she headed for the door herself. "And no matter how long you're here, you never, ever get to the bottom of the poop."

CHAPTER THIRTEEN

The houses on Oakdene Avenue were old and almost stately. They sat well back from the road on a bit of a slope, which made them even more imposing. Sasha trudged up the curved driveway with Tuni and checked her phone. The walk had taken exactly 14 minutes. She opened her purse and grabbed her props before going up the front stairs. Then she pressed the doorbell quickly, before she could chicken out.

The barking was loud and fierce, and she backed away before the inside door opened. The dog shoved his head through the opening and Sasha saw white fangs glinting.

"Rory, stop." An elegant woman wearing a taupe turtleneck and matching pants held the dog by the collar and looked up at Sasha. "Yes? How may I help you?"

"My name is Sasha Wildwood. I'm going door to door handing out flyers about the city's Valentine's Day event. We're recruiting participants for our contest."

The mayor hadn't confirmed a plan yet, but she'd keep the story as simple as her homemade flyer.

Rory calmed down so that his owner could stand up

straight and listen to Sasha's pitch for a Bachelor-style competition. "That sounds lovely, but I found my Valentine decades ago," she said. "Rory and I will have to pass."

"I understand, but I hope you'll at least join us on the 14th. There's nothing more romantic than celebrating your own romance by seeing someone else's begin."

The woman laughed. "Spoken like a true romantic. But I'm afraid Rory doesn't do well in a crowd. He's a handful."

"Aren't they all?" Sasha stared at the beautiful dog. "I've never met a ridgeback. Would you mind?"

The woman reached for his leash and hooked him up. Then she opened the door and came onto the porch in her slippers. Rory was a stunning brown dog with a darker face and a distinctive ridge of hair running down his spine. He was tall, leggy and 100 pounds, give or take. After giving Sasha's hand a cursory sniff, he turned his attention to Tuni. He maneuvered behind her quickly and prepared to mount her, but Tuni simply collapsed and rolled onto her back. If she hadn't been wearing a sweater, her condition would have been apparent.

"Oh, Rory," the woman said, pulling him back. "Boys will be boys, I guess. I wish my husband would let me get him fixed but he's got a phobia about it. And now the vet says the habit is probably ingrained anyway."

Rory circled Tuni looking for an access point and found none. His owner forced him into a sit and he stared at Tuni as if she were prey. For a moment he was motionless, but then he shook his head. And then he shook it again.

"How are his ears?" Sasha asked.

"What do you mean?"

"He's shaken his head a couple of times now, as if they're bothering him. Do you mind if I take a look?"

Sasha set her little black bag on the porch and opened it

to get her flashlight. The owner held Rory's collar with one hand so that Sasha could direct the light into his ear canal. Just as she'd suspected, there was a dark waxy substance. To confirm it, she leaned a little closer and sniffed. "It looks like Rory has an ear infection. You'll want to get that checked out soon, I think."

The woman's perfectly groomed eyebrows rose. "Oh my, I feel terrible I hadn't noticed. Thank you so much."

"It's always easier to see when you're meeting a dog for the first time. They made us study new dogs as part of my grooming program."

"Oh, you're a groomer. I guess that explains the kit. You come ready for anything."

Sasha smiled. "You never know when a grooming emergency might arise."

The woman asked for her card and she bid Rory good luck at the vet's before heading back home.

It seemed unlikely that Rory was Tuni's baby-daddy because he was more than three times her size and the logistics would have been awkward to say the least. If he was... well, her poor little pooch probably had a tough road ahead.

IT WAS 16 minutes to the next house at a steady trot. She assumed Tuni would have run most of the way to her suitor's house for their liaison. But Tuni herself gave no sign of being familiar with the house or the neighborhood. On the contrary, she gave signs of loving every house in every neighborhood. It was just her happy way.

Knocking on the door, Sasha got ready to deliver her Valentine's spiel again. It had worked beautifully on Mrs. Gunner, Rory's owner. But the man who opened the door didn't look nearly as disposed to romance. He had a big, unkempt beard and unruly frizzy hair.

By way of greeting, he simply said, "What?"

"Hello, I'm Sasha Wildwood. I'm here on behalf of—"

"Not interested," he said, starting to close the door. "Whatever you're selling."

"I'm not selling anything," she said. "I'm here on behalf of the City to—"

"Now I'm even less interested," he said. "I don't give a crap what the City wants you to say, no matter how pretty you are."

"I—uh—well, thank you."

"Thank me by leaving me in peace. I don't care about the City's stupid projects or causes. My dog and I are good without municipal interference."

"Of course you are," Sasha said. "It's not like that. I'm on the entertainment committee, nothing formal."

"Yikes, even worse." He pointed at Tuni. "I should have known by the sweater. It's a crime to do that to a good hound."

Sasha laughed. "I sort of agree with you there."

His beard seemed to bristle a little less. "Then why do it?"

"I'm a groomer and my business is cute dogs. What kind of dog do you have, if you don't mind my asking?"

"The kind that doesn't need a groomer."

"Short hair, then. Doesn't run in the hills. Doesn't roll in mud at the dog park. Does he just sit on a shelf and look handsome?"

Now the man was leaning against the doorframe, starting to enjoy himself. "Pretty much, these days. He doesn't run in the hills anymore because he's thirteen."

"Thirteen! You've done well." She gestured to Tuni. "I'd be thrilled to get another twelve with this one."

The man moved out of the doorway and revealed an old boxer standing behind him. The dog's muzzle was completely silver, but his bug eyes were bright. "He's a good boy. And he gets up happy every day, even if he's a little stiff."

A little stiff was an understatement. When he opened the door to let the old boxer out, the dog moved carefully, as if considering every step. He greeted her politely, but actually backed away from Tuni, as if he feared her exuberance.

There was no way this elderly gentleman had the energy or coordination to pull off the deed.

In other words, bachelor number two seemed as unlikely as number one. If her sources were correct, that left only one known stud living within a reasonable run for Tuni from her backyard escape hatch.

And if bachelor number three was the puppy-daddy, Tuni was in big trouble.

THE HOUSE WAS much nicer than she expected. In fact, she hadn't really expected a house. He didn't look like the kind of guy who'd choose to live in a sweet little cottage with urns filled with pine boughs, now dropping their needles on the snow. The lights were still strung over a skinny birch beside the front stairs. White like everyone else's. Nothing radical here.

"Must be the wrong address," she muttered to Tuni. "But we'll give it a try."

Tuni walked ahead of her up the stairs, tail wagging. Sasha tried to read a story into that tail but knew it meant nothing more than that a dog lived there. Dogs lived almost everywhere and Tuni existed in a state of perpetual hope that she'd meet a new playmate. Maybe that's what she thought she was doing that day... just playing with a fun dog. There was no way she could—

"Anthropomorphizing," she said, loud enough to make Tuni turn. "Time to stop that."

Taking a deep breath, she pressed the doorbell. A moment later, the curtains moved and then the inside door opened.

"Well, well, well," Griffin Granger said, through the glass outer door. "The groomer makes house calls."

"I do, actually, for the right client." She looked down at his feet for signs of Grover. "You're not the right client."

He raised one tattooed, muscular arm and leaned against the doorway, smiling. It was more of a smirk than a smile, but there were teeth, and they were even and white. The smile made him look less likely to graffiti a public building, but there was still the matter of his bald head. She didn't understand that choice. What was he hiding by not hiding?

"And yet here you are at my door," he said. "I'd almost think you had a crush—" She opened her mouth to protest and he continued, "On Grover."

"Well, that much is true. He's a charmer and definitely my type."

"And maybe Tuni's, as well."

She pulled in a sharp breath of cold air. "What do you mean?"

"I've tried to tell you. Twice. But you didn't want to hear."

"Didn't want to hear *what*?"

He opened the door so that the glass wasn't between

them. "That Tuni's been hanging around here. The first time I thought it could have been any type of spaniel. The second time I noticed the purple plaid collar. There may be other Welsh springer spaniels wearing that particular plaid, but it's a long shot."

"She's been hanging around here? Twice?"

"Three times that I know of. Probably more. She comes in the afternoon and I'm not always around."

"Really?" Her voice was squeaky with shock. "To see Grover?"

He crossed his arms and for the first time she saw that the tattoo on his right wrist was a brindle English bulldog. "I assume so. But Grover is never outside on his own."

"Too cold," she said. "With his respiratory problems."

"That, too. But I'd never just leave him out. You don't know what could happen."

Sasha put two and two together. "Because he's not neutered. He could cause trouble."

Griffin stared at her, his green eyes unblinking. "He doesn't, though. Not even when other dogs come *looking* for trouble. Tuni isn't spayed, is she?"

"Why do you ask?"

"I was kneeling beside her at the vet and I know the signs. My parents never spayed Honey, their golden retriever."

She glanced around to make sure no one was listening. Of course, she was the only one gadding about on the coldest day of the winter so far. "No," she said at last. "Tuni isn't spayed. I booked it twice and she was too sick for surgery. And now it's too late."

"Too late for what?"

"Too late to lock the barn. The horse already bolted."

He opened the door wider and stepped out onto the porch in his bare feet. "Are you saying she's pregnant?"

"Hush. Do you think that's something I want to get around? People judge, Griffin."

He smirked again. "Yeah, they do. Including you."

"Well, you think I'm an irresponsible owner because my dog came here looking for... looking for love."

"Poor Tuni found only heartbreak and loneliness here. So she must have kept running."

Tears beaded on her eyelashes and froze in the icy wind. "Don't joke about this. It's... it's tragic."

"Puppies are never tragic," he said, and this time all his perfect teeth flashed. "Puppies are better than Christmas. My parents bred Honey once and we practically held a parade. Everyone from miles around came to see the puppies."

"I assume those were purebred retrievers. My pups will be tragic. They'll have huge bulldog heads on tiny spaniel bodies."

He hopped from one foot to the other. "They're not Grover's. Even if he were outside—which he wasn't—he wouldn't have the first clue."

"I would have said the same thing about Tuni. But when my landlord let her out for me, she dug her way under the fence and followed her instincts."

"Yeah, but bulldogs are notoriously inept when it comes to breeding. It doesn't happen without artificial insemination."

"I don't believe you."

"Look it up," he said, stepping back inside. "I'm sorry to hear about this and I wish you the best. But it really isn't the end of the world. She'll have puppies, you'll find good homes for them and it'll be like this never happened."

She turned and started down the stairs. "What planet are you from? My reputation in Dog Town will be ruined and my business will go under."

"You're overreacting, like usual," he called after her. "And Dog Town is stupid anyway."

CHAPTER FOURTEEN

It should have been harder to climb into Griffin's yard, given that her fingers could barely move from the cold, but fury had warmed her and sent blood through her limbs. Pushing through the hedge surrounding the fence had been hard, and she had scratches on her face to prove it. Once she saw the hole, she was determined enough to see the other side that the climb seemed easy. After tying Tuni's leash to a hook on his garage, she flipped his trash can, stepped into the crook of the apple tree, swung out on a bough and dropped down on the other side.

For a moment, she forgot why she was there. She'd landed hard enough to steal her breath, and when it came back she thought she'd arrived in another Santa's village, this one filled with small wooden houses of various shapes, sizes and colors. Doghouses, she realized, when her heart rate steadied. There were dozens of them, some stacked like two-storey homes for upscale elves.

Remembering her mission, she walked over to a large shed with gingerbread trim that looked like Santa's own dwelling. Behind it, she found the evidence: claw marks on the inside of the fence. Deep grooves that could only be caused by a dog far bigger than Tuni.

She took a picture with her phone, but it wasn't necessary. By the time she emerged, the sliding door on the deck was open. Griffin took the back stairs at a single bound and charged towards her as fast as his big, unlaced boots could carry him.

"What the hell are you doing in my yard?" he asked.

"Trying to figure out how a dog that never goes outside unsupervised clawed his way to freedom." She gestured behind the shed. "Take a look for yourself. In the meantime, I'm going to collect Tuni."

She unlocked the gate and then came back in with the dog. Without waiting for an invitation, she walked into Griffin's house.

"Make yourself at home," he grumbled. "Tuni obviously has."

"I won't let my dog freeze while you continue this charade. Only Grover could cause that damage to the fence. Big powerful claws, and fairly recent, too. So my dog isn't the only one following instincts."

He paced in the kitchen, running his hands over his bald head, one after the other. "This is impossible."

Perching on an old oak chair at a matching table, she said, "Think back. Weekend of December 15th. Afternoon. What were you doing?"

He stopped and stared into space, and then realization rushed in. Color surged up from his collar and whooshed right over his scalp. "Christmas craft show in Milverton. My friend stayed with Grover, and he knows better than to—"

"Just like my landlord knows better. So. Mystery solved. We're expecting."

He sat across from her, looking disoriented. "Grover doesn't know how."

"None of us initially knows how, yet babies—and puppies—happen all the time."

A mischievous grin flashed across Griffin's face. "I guess we all figure it out, don't we?"

His grin caused a little pinging sound in her head. A warning. Grins like that did no good for anyone, especially her. "Well," she said. "We're talking about Grover, anyway."

"He wouldn't. He's not that kind of dog."

Sasha actually laughed. "I guess I'm not the only one anthropomorphizing. But like the vet told me, they're just animals."

He waved dismissively. "It's not like that. I know my dog."

"Yeah? Well, what is he doing now? The tango?"

Grover had circled Tuni and maneuvered into the driver's seat.

"Grover, stop!" Griffin sounded shocked.

Tuni slithered away and raced out of the kitchen. She was no longer in the mood for funny business.

"What do you say now?" Sasha asked.

"Wow," he said at last. "If this... If he... Wow. These would be... interesting... puppies."

"Ugly, you mean."

"Grover isn't ugly. You said yourself he's adorable."

"That was before I knew he violated my dog. Now I'll say he's ugly. Adorable, but ugly."

Tuni raced back in, with Grover close behind. He missed her and charged into the cabinets.

"See? He's a klutz. There's no way he could have pulled this off."

"Think what you like. I'll let my vet know that Tuni's in for a tough delivery of cranially challenged pups."

Resting his elbows on the table, he rubbed his eyes and forehead. "Isn't there any other option?"

She shook her head. "Not now. It's past the midway point and the vet says it's dangerous. Even if it weren't I don't think I could do it."

"Can we get a DNA test to prove Grover's the dad? I mean, it would be good to know what she's in for, right? I'll pay for it."

Suddenly blood pounded in her ears, and she rose. It was her dog and she didn't need his help.

"No thank you. I don't need your money. I just wanted to know what I was dealing with. Now I do." She walked through the living room to the front door. The furniture was typical of any man cave, with a dark leather couch too big for the room, a recliner too big for any room but a movie theater, and a TV screen taking up half the wall. So his appearance was just a facade. He was no more rebellious than she was.

"Sasha, wait," he said. "Let's talk about this. I want to do the right thing."

She opened the door, yanking Tuni behind her. Lawrence, her fiancé, had said exactly the same thing before he left her behind in Dorset Hills.

Running down the front stairs, she fired back, "Total cliché. None of you mean it—not even Grover."

THE CANE almost tripped her as she rushed past.

"Devil after you?" Bart asked, when she stopped.

"I think so," she panted. "Yes."

"Big guy? You don't know whether to laugh or scream?"

"Exactly. You've seen him, too."

Bart chuckled. "You get to my age, you've seen everything. But you don't get used to seeing a young lady upset."

Sasha forced a smile. "I'm okay, Bart. It's just been a heck of a week. I'm a bit flustered."

He stumped on, and she forced herself to slow down to his pace although she ached to start running again. She was only a block from home now. Her basement dungeon would be a welcome refuge.

"Getting flustered is a waste of energy," Bart said. "You get more judicious about how you spend it when you're older."

"Well, I've got a lot going on, you know. With the salon. And everything else."

"You're making a mountain out of a molehill."

She stared at him, wondering what he knew. "It's a mountain. Or at least a very large hill."

He stepped around Tuni, who was cavorting for Puck's benefit and getting nowhere. "They're all molehills, and you'll see that in time."

Her heart slowed, and her breathing returned to normal. "I hope you're right."

"Of course I'm right. Every time you doubt, I want you to look at the mascot I gave you and take a deep breath. Just like you're doing now. Remind yourself that all will be well."

"But what if it isn't?"

He gave her a look over his glasses. "All will be well. Unless you fly off the handle."

She pushed the hat out of her eyes. "Deep breaths. Look at stuffed dog. Remind self all will be well."

"Exactly." His eyes crinkled. "I knew you could get this."

She pulled in another lungful of prickly cold air. "Okay. Can I make you a coffee, Bart?"

"No thanks. Puck and I can only handle you two in small doses." He smiled to take away the sting. "But we do like you, young lady. And you're going to turn out just fine."

CHAPTER FIFTEEN

"Really, Sasha," Mike said. "Please get up. This is unnecessary."

"It'll just take a minute," she said, from the floor at Mike's feet. "I want to."

There was a murmur around the meeting room at City Hall, and then a cluck of disapproval. Ignoring it, Sasha grabbed the clippers from the little black bag she took everywhere now, and quickly snipped the claws of Mike's mix-breed bulldog. The click of claws over the old building's hardwood floors had been driving her crazy. It set off an internal groomer alarm.

It really did take only a minute, because the dog was so placid. He was one of Bridget's rescues, she knew. When she was done, she accepted the hand Mike offered and scrambled to her feet. The rest of the committee was frowning at her. They probably thought she was sucking up to Mike, but they didn't understand. She liked things neat, tidy and even. Precision had been drilled into her during years of hairstyling and now it had morphed into a new obsession.

Remi walked into the room just as Mike released her hand. Her eyebrows went up but she just smiled as Sasha brushed dust off her black dress pants. She'd worn boots with a nice heel and her favorite pink wool coat. It was like armor against the stares of the old guard. *Fake it till you make it*, she reminded herself.

"Now that we're all here, let's get straight to business," Mike said. "At Marsha's request, I put forward the plan for the dog beauty contest, and Mayor Bradshaw asked us to come up with something more... vibrant."

"Vibrant?" Marsha said. "What does that mean exactly?"

Mike perched on a table at the front of the room. "In the mayor's own words, he's looking for 'wow factor.' He wants to give people something to look forward to in the middle of the February doldrums."

"You mean he's rattled about this dog court business," Marsha said. "I hear Marti Forester left this week."

Mike raised ginger eyebrows. "All politicians want good press. It goes with the territory. The mayor's worried the same old beauty contest won't attract much attention."

"Same old?" Marsha' voice crackled with indignation. "This is what tradition looks like. We need stability in trying times. People like to know what to expect."

Mike shrugged. "All I can tell you is that the mayor wants something fresh. 'Not stodgy,' were his exact words."

Marsha reared back so hard her chair nearly tipped. "Stodgy! That's a terrible thing to say. This town is built on traditions like the Valentine's Day beauty contest."

"That was old Dog Town," Mike said. "New Dog Town needs a facelift. I'm going to be frank. The mayor wants something on par with the Thanksgiving Rescue Pageant. Something newsworthy. He wants to hire a camera crew and shoot a video and share it with news stations across the country."

"We only have three weeks," Marsha said. "What can we do in three weeks?"

Mike smiled. "Lots. Because if the mayor likes our pitch, he's willing to get us into the Elgin Theater. Imagine what we can do with that venue."

There was a collective gasp. "The Elgin?" Remi said. "We'd be inside. We'll have a stage."

"And a budget for props," Mike said. "He wants this to look high-end."

Sasha raised her hand tentatively, and when Mike nodded, she said, "The Bachelor and Bachelorette, Dog Town Edition."

The murmur of disapproval started again, but Mike spoke over it. "I'm listening."

"We recruit single women and men and their dogs. They dress in matching black tie formal and come down the runway. People vote on a male winner and a female. The winning pair—and their dogs, of course—get a super romantic dinner. It would have to be a great prize to get people to participate."

"Too similar to the Thanksgiving Rescue Pageant," Marsha said. "The mayor wouldn't go for that. It's direct competition."

"I think he might," Mike said, getting up. "Let me make a call."

"That's exactly what the mayor wants," Remi whispered to Sasha when Mike was gone. "He's hoping to compete directly with Bridget's pageant and catch more media attention with a glitzy venue, beautiful people in formal dress and fundraising for service dogs."

"I didn't want to compete with Bridget's pageant,"

Sasha said.

"Don't worry about that," Remi said. "In Dog Town, it's never a zero sum game. People will come out and support everything. By next November, they'll be ready for more rescue magic."

Mike came back and pumped his arm. "The win goes to Sasha. The Valentine's singles contest is a go."

A flutter of excitement stirred in Sasha's chest. Maybe her luck was turning again, and she could generate some business from this. There were costs now she hadn't anticipated, including fostering Tuni for months, and additional vet bills related to pregnancy and puppies. She was going to end up with debt. The only question was how much.

"Maybe the mayor could participate," she suggested. "That would certainly add spice to the event."

Mike laughed. "Well, I doubt that. I'll leave it to him."

"I guess it wouldn't be a fair contest," Sasha said. "Everyone would vote for him as premier bachelor of Dog Town."

"Or not," Remi whispered. "And that would be worse."

Sasha smothered a laugh and then asked, "What about the prize? It has to be spectacular to attract the best bachelors and bachelorettes."

"That's where we're on our own," Mike said. "The mayor doesn't want to be seen favoring any local business."

Marsha turned to Sasha, her lips pressed together in a pained smile. "I'm sure our eager new friend can come up with a spectacular prize. She seems to have all the answers."

"Now, now, the whole committee is responsible," Mike said. "We're a team."

As they walked out together, Remi said, "We're always a team when everything goes according to the old guard's plan. When it doesn't, it's every dog for herself."

THE LIME-GREEN VAN was idling in a no-standing zone outside City Hall when the meeting ended. Other drivers honked, and a black glove with a neon orange middle finger came out the driver's window and waved.

"I wish I could come," Remi said, as they walked down the wide stone stairs. "But you'll be in good hands."

Sasha glanced down at Tuni, who as always was greeting life with a sweeping tail. "I hope they're right about this woman," she said. "The name Doggie Doula doesn't exactly inspire confidence."

"Cori and Bridget would never steer you wrong on dog care," Remi said. "But trust your gut. If you don't like her, they'll find someone else."

Sasha's butt had barely settled into the back seat before Cori put the pedal to the floor. "We've only got two hours so I'm driving."

"Try to keep the van in one piece," Bridget said. "I can't afford to replace it until after next year's pageant."

Sasha told them about the plan for the Valentine's gala. "I hope this doesn't compete with your pageant too much."

"It won't, because it's stupid," Cori said.

"It was my idea," Sasha said.

"You don't have to *be* stupid to have a stupid idea that the mayor jumps all over."

"I guess you won't be participating, then," Sasha said. "What a waste of the fabulous haircut I gave you."

Cori offered her right hand and waggled the neon middle finger. "You used to be kind of sweet. I liked that about you."

"You never like sweet," Bridget said, laughing. "Hence your visceral reaction to the romance of Valentine's Day.

But once you find true love, as I have, you'll change your tune."

The neon flipping finger moved into a gagging position. "Don't make me feel sicker than this town already does."

Bridget turned from the passenger seat. "Don't worry, Sasha. There's more than enough goodwill to go around for events like this. I'm happy you're getting in there and participating. It can only help your business."

"The mayor's just desperate to divert attention from the travesty of dog court," Cori said. "I've been working nearly fulltime to bring that down. With Marti Forrester leaving, it'll probably get worse."

"I think it will crumble soon," Bridget said. "Marti was put in an awkward position by the mayor and now he's trying to hang her out to dry. People aren't stupid."

"Most are," Cori said. "Marti was stupid to say yes in the first place. That said, I like her. She's not the first person to get churned up in the Dog Town meatgrinder and she won't be the last."

"I hope the next one isn't me," Sasha said.

"That's why we're developing our plan early," Cori said, as they sped down the highway toward Milverton.

"You're going to like Devina," Bridget said. "She's fun and smart and her heart's in the right place. She moved out of Dorset Hills when the mayor got voted in. Now she fosters a good few of our dogs. Her experience as a breeder means she can take in pregnant rescues, which has been helpful."

Half an hour later, they were sitting in Devina's living room, surrounded by half a dozen rescues of various shapes and sizes. Devina herself wasn't at all what Sasha expected. She was probably close to 70 and impeccably groomed, with a great haircut and lowlights.

Tuni took to Devina. With no coaxing at all, she rolled on her back in her pink parka and offered her belly.

Devina accepted the invitation to poke around. "Feels like a good-sized litter," she said. "I hope you're getting an ultrasound so we have a better sense of what to expect."

Sasha nodded. "The vet said it would be more accurate when she's past 40 days. So I'll take her in next week."

She shared her fears about Grover with them. "What if the puppies have massive heads and get stuck in there?"

"First, there's no way to know for sure it's this Grover."

"It's him," Sasha said. "He'd dug under his fence to get out, or let her in."

"You'd be surprised," Bridget said. "Even if they did the deed, it doesn't mean it took. Bulldogs are notoriously hard to breed, right Devi?"

Devi nodded. "So I've heard. No matter who the sire is, it will all be fine, I'm sure. I've delivered at least forty litters in the last ten years with only rare complications. For those times, we have the vet on call and he'll do a caesarian."

Sasha winced at the thought. "I'm so worried about her."

"I know you are, but she'll be perfectly safe here, I promise."

Bridget and Cori both nodded encouragingly and Sasha reluctantly agreed to bring Tuni back well in advance of her due date.

Cori's phone buzzed and she jumped to her feet. "It's a 911. Let's deploy."

"Do you need me?" Devina asked. "I've still got my rescue chops."

"No worries," Cori said, heading for the door. "We've got Sasha."

"YOU COULD HAVE MENTIONED I'd need cleats," Sasha said, sliding after Bridget and Cori down the path beside the old barn. The sun was low now and the wind had whipped up. A gust blew a sheet of fine snow into her face and blinded her temporarily.

"I offered you my spare boots," Cori said, forging ahead.

"They're child-sized," Sasha said.

"Duff pulls off rescues in heels, so quit complaining. You'll be fine. And then you won't wear heels again."

"I'll always wear heels. Part of my job is looking polished."

"You're a dog groomer now, not a hair stylist."

Sasha sighed. "I'm still making the transition, I guess."

"All you have to do is stand sentry," Bridget said. "We'll go in, grab the dog, and get out fast. Only use the flashlight if you have to."

When they reached the barn, Bridget cracked opened the big door, and Cori slipped inside. A second later she was back. "The dog's feral from neglect. Bee, I need help."

Bridget went in with her, and the thumping inside was alarming. There was no sign of life at the house, so Sasha finally joined them.

They'd cornered the dog at the back of its wooden pen, and were murmuring to it in calm voices. The whites of the dog's eyes and its bared teeth showed in the circle of Sasha's flashlight. The poor thing was painfully thin and shivering from terror and cold. It was too far gone to take the treats they offered, or even let them get near enough to touch it.

Circling the pen, Sasha got behind the dog.

"Don't move," Cori said. "We're finally making headway."

Sasha set her black bag on the dirty floor and fished around till she found what she wanted. "Distract the dog," she said. "Move your hands to the left, Bridget. Now."

Bridget followed directions. Sasha leaned over the pen, slipped the loop of her grooming noose over the dog's muzzle and tightened it swiftly. Cori quickly slid a burlap sack over the dog and Sasha dropped the noose. The poor dog let out a muffled, heartrending screech.

"Let's go," Sasha hissed. She shone the light to the door and then turned it off.

The dog thrashed in the sack over Cori's shoulder for the first few yards and then gave up. Its stillness was somehow more tragic than the fight. Sasha hoped it would hang in till the Mafia could give it a good life... the life any pet deserved.

She fell three times on the way back to the van and considered herself lucky.

When they were on the highway again, Cori said, "That was a very risky move, Sasha." Keeping her left hand on the wheel, she stuck her right hand through the seats for a high five. "Good job." The orange finger fluttered before she pulled back her hand. "But don't let it go to your head."

"Unlikely," Sasha said. "My coat is wrecked, my ankle's swelling and my butt is wet and freezing. That'll keep my ego in check."

"Just the beginning, my friend," Cori said. She actually started humming as she drove. It sounded like *We Are the Champions*. "Soon you and your grooming noose will be leading the charge."

CHAPTER SIXTEEN

Remi and Leo had come to open The Model Dog on Sunday so that the first client could drop off her dog on time. Sasha was running late after a christening ceremony, where she'd wrangled the family's two dogs through the hour-long photo shoot.

"You look good," Remi said, as Sasha pushed open the door and rushed in on a stiff breeze.

"It's so hard to know how to dress for something like that," Sasha said. "You want to fit in with the other guests, yet you need to be prepared for dog fur, pawprints and slobber. There were two St. Bernards. I deserved a better tip."

"You'll get lots of business out of it, I bet," Remi said.

"I hope so, because my costs are on the rise." She perched on the pew so that Tuni could get at her without jumping. Remi had picked Tuni up from Sasha's apartment and chosen her outfit: a tiny christening dress with slits for the legs and tail. "Oh my goodness, she looks like a bride."

"A child bride, which she is," Remi said, grinning.

"Isn't it blasphemous to cut holes in a christening dress?"

"They were already there. I picked it up at Vintage Vixen, along with half a dozen other outfits. I have to admit, it was fun shopping for Tuni. She's like my honorary niece."

"Or maybe the little girl you want," Sasha said.

Remi flushed a pretty pink. "Someday. I hope. How about you? Do you want kids?"

"I'm not sure." She bent over to thread Tuni's tail through the right opening. "For now it's just Tuni, me and Devina the Doggie Doula."

"It sounds like a decent set up." Remi sat down at the other end of the pew. "What did you think?"

"I liked Devi. She has the experience and Tuni seemed happy there. I guess that's what counts." Straightening her shoulders, she smiled. "Did you hear what happened afterward?"

"About your brave exploits in the barn? Oh yes. It traveled the rescue grapevine very quickly. Cori was impressed. I don't think I need to tell you how rare that is."

Sasha laughed. "That probably shouldn't mean as much as it does."

"I care about her good opinion, too. She's like the conscience of Dog Town—the sniff test of all that stinks around here."

"That sounds about right. I finally felt vindicated. I get teased so much about my travel grooming kit, but at last it came in handy."

"You never know when you're going to need a noose."

"It's not even the first time I wanted to use it."

Their laughter cut off as the doorbells chimed. In walked Rory, the Rhodesian ridgeback, and his owner, Mrs. Gunner. She was wearing a Prada coat, and the dog was, too—or at least a very good knockoff. Whatever the designer, Sasha noted an odd detail: the tail end of the coat had a flap that closed under the belly with Velcro. It would keep out a stiff January breeze nicely, but it would also prevent the dog from doing his business. Mrs. Gunner didn't seem like the type to be constantly opening and closing the output chute, let alone cleaning up if Rory fired too soon.

Jumping to her feet, Sasha greeted Mrs. Gunner with an outstretched hand. The woman offered Sasha a leather glove so soft and fine it felt like satin.

"How are you, my dear? I just stopped by to thank you. You were right about Rory's ear. We've come from a follow-up at the vet and he's doing well. I'd like to invite you to the house to groom him. He's more comfortable at home."

Rory looked totally comfortable standing over Tuni, who'd rolled onto her back. Entirely too comfortable, actually, as he poked his snout where it didn't belong. Luckily Remi got up to join them and nudged Tuni deliberately with her boot till she rolled right side up.

"I'd love to do a home visit for Rory," Sasha said. "I'm just starting to offer that service."

"Wonderful. I have a grooming room, of course."

Remi offered her hand and Sasha grinned at her surprised expression when she felt the satiny glove. "This is my friend, Remi Malone," she said.

"We've met at fundraising events, Mrs. Gunner," Remi said. "I work for the hospital foundation."

"Plus, Remi and I are working together on the Valentine's Day event I told you about, Sasha said.

Mrs. Gunner smiled. "Still not interested, I'm afraid."

Figuring she had nothing to lose, Sasha said, "Would you consider donating a prize? We're trying to round up a romantic dinner or two."

"There isn't enough romance around Dorset Hills these

days," Remi said. "It dried up when things went to the dogs."

"I couldn't agree more," Mrs. Gunner said. "When Vance and I were your age, there were so many quaint bistros. Now for special occasions we head to the outskirts. The Wychwood Mill is a wonderful conversion. Have you tried it?"

"Not yet, but I'd love to," Remi said.

"I'd be dining alone, I'm afraid," Sasha said. "The opposite of romance."

"Oh Sasha, we must find you a nice young man," Mrs. Gunner said. "You're so pretty, and your Tuni is adorable. Truly a model dog."

"Thank you, Mrs. Gunner. So... what do you say about the donation?"

"Persistent, isn't she?" Mrs. Gunner asked Remi. "And I suppose I'll start hearing from you on behalf of the hospital foundation?"

"Worthy causes, both of them," Remi said, smiling.

"Well, I can't say no to committed young women like you. So full of zeal for this silly town that it's contagious. Dinner for two it is, with a nice bottle of champagne, some roses for the lucky lady, and a nice meal for their dogs as well."

Sasha actually clapped. "That's amazing! The mayor will be so pleased."

"Now, now, don't ruin my mood," Mrs. Gunner said. "Bill Bradshaw and I don't see eye to eye on much, I'm afraid. This dog court, fiasco... Honestly." She turned and opened the door. "When I get a moment with him, Rory won't be the only one with sore ears."

Remi and Sasha watched Mrs. Gunner walk down the sidewalk, gasping as she nearly slipped on the ever-present ice patch. Rory tried to lift his leg on a hydrant and she jerked the leash to stop him.

When she was out of sight, Remi said, "Well done, Sasha. Things are coming together now. The universe works in mysterious ways, doesn't it?"

"Mysterious indeed." She pulled a smock from under the counter and slipped it over her nice clothes. "What's not mysterious at all is the Russian blue terrier awaiting his bath. Thanks again for pinch-hitting for me today. It's hard to be everywhere at once."

"My pleasure, truly," Remi said, gathering her things. "Where else do I get to sit around and have rare dogs come to me? I thought I'd miss the boardwalk in winter, but now I have The Model Dog."

"Leo's always a model dog," Sasha said, waving goodbye.

The dog was soaked and soaped in the tub when the bells rang. She'd forgotten to lock the door again.

"Hello!" she called. There was no answer so she left the grooming room and poked her head around the corner. A clean-cut man in a navy pea jacket stood at the counter.

"Am I interrupting something?" he asked, smiling.

Sasha suddenly realized she was not only wearing a baggy wet smock, but also a plastic shower cap. Most dogs accepted the shower with resignation, but not this big baby. He'd been shaking and shivering till the entire grooming room was doused.

Snatching off the plastic cap, she came to the counter. "May I help you?"

"Possibly. Are you Sasha Wildwood, the proprietor?"

"I am, yes." She searched his face for clues. He'd looked more handsome than he actually was. Up close, she could see that his features weren't particularly nice. Then again, he had a fine head of shiny dark hair, and that went a long way.

Still smiling, he offered her an envelope. "I work with the City, and I've been asked to deliver some information."

"About the Valentine's Day bachelor gala?"

His eyebrows rose. "Uh, no. Must be another division."

The envelope wilted in her hand from the dampness. "I have a dog in the tub. Could I read this later?"

"Of course. But you may have questions that I'd be happy to answer." He took the envelope back. "Allow me."

He pulled a white sheet of paper about two-thirds of the way out and handed it back.

Sasha scanned it quickly. "It's from the Canine Corrections Department. It says The Model Dog has been found in violation of municipal bylaws."

His brown eyes were sympathetic. "I'm afraid so."

"Which bylaws?" She scanned the rest of the page. "It doesn't list anything."

"It's just a warning letter, don't look so worried," he said.

"Of course I'm worried. I only just opened and I'm getting a warning? This is terrible."

"Don't get the wrong idea. The CCD is here to help dog-business owners like you, not scare them."

"But what have I done wrong? I looked up the regulations for groomers and checked every box. I'm diligent that way."

"I'm sure you are, Ms. Wildwood. These aren't the worse of the infractions by any means. But take today, for example. You had someone who isn't on your payroll receiving a dog from an owner. And when I came in just now, there was no one out front. Anything could have happened with dogs on the premises."

"You're spying on me?"

"Not spying... observing. To make sure dogs are safe in Dorset Hills. We had reason to think things weren't all they could be."

"Reason to think? Did someone complain?"

"If they did, I couldn't say. But I confirmed today with my own eyes that there's too little supervision on the premises during hours of operation. I recommend hiring reliable staff."

"Staff? I can't afford staff. Do you have any idea how expensive it is to—"

"Absolutely we do. But it would be a shame to run into difficulty over something so easily remedied."

"By trained staff I can't afford and don't need."

"Clearly you do. It seems that business is booming, and you're in a prime location. There's no question you'll thrive here... if you pay attention to the details."

"Are you saying I could lose this location?"

His bland expression got even blander. "I've already said I'm here to help. This is just an on-site visit to help a new business owner get on her feet."

"But I—"

"Don't get yourself upset, Ms. Wildwood. For the moment, keep your mind on the task at hand. Unless I'm much mistaken, there's a dog alone in the tub back there. Perhaps leashed and at risk of drowning."

"What a terrible thing to say! I would never—"

"Don't worry, this is just between us." He smiled again and he really did look well-intentioned. "Just lock the door when I leave, put the shower cap back on—it's a nice touch—and get that dog to safety before its owner returns."

"But I need more information about my supposed infractions. How am I supposed to address them?"

"Take care of the dog. Later, review your operations and think about what I've said. Then by all means—" he flipped a card onto the counter "—give me a call."

She stood watching, shower cap dangling from her fingertips, as he let himself out. He signaled for her to lock the door, and then gave a merry wave as he walked off into the snow.

All day people had been sliding on the icy sidewalk, but not CCD inspector Rodney Crump. He had complete command of his treads.

CHAPTER SEVENTEEN

The next morning, she opened the salon long before dawn and inspected every nook and cranny. As far as she could tell, there was nothing that did not meet or surpass municipal requirements for a grooming operation. In fact, the rules for groomers were few; almost anyone who had money and common sense could run a dog salon. She'd done a lot of research and gathered best practices from the instructors of the well-respected grooming program she'd taken. It seemed impossible that she was in violation of municipal codes. Surely the letter would have been more prescriptive if that were true.

Just before nine, she came out of the back with Tuni and saw someone standing outside the door. The person was hooded and wrapped up in scarves. Her hands clutched a walker.

Running to the door, Sasha ushered the woman inside. "Carole! It's good to see you up and around, but is it safe to be using a walker alone? It's terribly icy."

Carole pushed her hood back and smiled. "It feels great

to be out on my own. My granddaughter was starting to annoy me with her constant orders."

Sasha laughed. "She only wants the best for you, I'm sure."

"Well, I'm recovering quicker than anyone expected. One doctor said I'd never walk again, you know. And look at me!"

She did a slow, stiff pirouette that made Sasha hold her breath. "Careful now."

"You're worried I'll fall and sue you?" Carole laughed. "I had a few ladies slip on shampoo over the years and threaten to sue. They never did, though. Too much trouble."

"I'm sure you wouldn't sue me. But I admit there's more to running a business than I expected."

Carole lowered herself onto the pew. "You can't be everywhere at once, for starters. I'd be washing out color and someone would check the curling iron to see if it really was hot enough to leave a scar. It was."

"I figured dogs were easier to control than humans. I leash and use crates and baby gates, but I wonder if it's enough."

"The difference is the culture here," Carole said. "Dogs are more important than humans in Dorset Hills. I bet you charge more for grooming than I ever did for a haircut."

"Well, I charge more than I ever did for hair, so probably."

"I've come by a couple of times and the shop was closed," Carole said. "I hear you do house calls."

"And other events. I'm trying to drum up business so I say yes to everything."

"But you're losing walk-ins, my dear. I think you need part-time help."

"I wish I could afford that," Sasha said. "I need more income, not less."

"Having the right help will free you to chase leads. You just need someone who's willing to work flexible hours for nearly nothing. Minimum wage and monthly grooming."

"I doubt I'd find anyone willing to do that," Sasha said.

Carole lifted her hand. "I volunteer. Well, not volunteer. Like I said, minimum wage and monthly grooming for Caesar. My schedule is completely flexible."

"But why, Carole? Are you sure you'd feel comfortable coming back here?"

The older woman gazed around. She'd given herself a perm, it seemed, and Sasha had to agree it held up well.

"I miss the place," Carole said. "I miss the people. I miss looking across the street and seeing what silly Lotus Fiore is doing at Crackers." She turned back and smiled. "But I don't miss the responsibility, or the worry, or backbreaking labor. By helping you out, I could get the best of both worlds."

"That is such a kind offer. Let me think about how I'd afford it," Sasha said.

"Take your time. I've made a similar offer at The Lucky Dog Barkery and Small Wonders boutique. Something is bound to work out."

Sasha knew it was a pressure tactic, but she fell for it anyway. Having Carole on board would go a long way to addressing the concerns of Officer Crump. If he came back —*when* he came back—he'd find someone on duty even if she wasn't. The dogs and the storefront would never be left unattended. What's more, Carole was the previous owner, who knew the building, the neighbors and a lot of the clients. Now that she thought about it, hiring Carole was a great idea. It might mean she never had to tell the Mafia about the dog cop's visit. The last thing she wanted to do was worry them, when they'd been so good to her.

"When can you start, Carole?" she asked.

"I brought my lunch," she said, smiling. "I had a feeling we'd hit it off."

"Perfect. Because I have my first official house call, and someone will be dropping off her schnauzer at 11, so it would have been tight. Let's make sure you can get around with your walker. I'd hate to think a dog could knock you over again."

"Lightning doesn't strike twice," Carole said. "Get your coat and go scare up more business."

THE ICE PATCH OUT front was a malignant force that caught Sasha every day, no matter how careful she was. Leaving the shop in a hurry today, her arms pinwheeled and her feet slid wildly. Suddenly a cane came out and she caught it. Bart was holding a lamppost and pulled her to safety.

"What did I tell you?" he said.

"Deep breaths," she said. "Remind myself all will be well."

"I also said pay attention. You're running straight into trouble that's easily avoided."

"This ice patch gets bigger every day no matter how much salt I put on it. Or salt-substitute. We can't hurt the dogs' paws, but it's okay for humans to go flying."

"I walk by every day without mishap. All I do is pay attention."

She laughed. "Point taken, Bart. There's just so much going on."

"It's important to develop a skillful mind."

"Does this require some sort of mental calisthenics? Because I don't have time for that, either."

He tipped back his fedora to see her better. "Just be curious. Question everything. Listen to your intuition."

"But never worry. Or make mountains out of molehills."

"A skillful mind is more helpful than anything you've got in your little black bag."

"Understood," she said. "At least, I think so. You're a man of many riddles, Bart."

"Slip off for your appointment," he said, giving her a little jab between the shoulder blades. "I've got your back."

CHAPTER EIGHTEEN

The old house was large, but nothing like the mansion Sasha had expected. She assumed only wealthy dog owners would foot the bill for home grooming. It was double the price of a cut in the shop, partly because she had to bring so much equipment with her. The grooming table alone took up the entire back seat of her car.

A woman in floral surgical scrubs and a nametag from a home care service met her at the door, and took her inside to meet the owner. Mrs. Barber, an elderly woman, was in a recliner covered by a crocheted afghan. On top of that sat a pretty, deep-red poodle.

"This is Garnet," Mrs. Barber said. "She's a purebred poodle with papers, but I really don't like her to look like one. Does that make any sense?"

Her laugh was light and infectious. No matter what health problems she struggled with, it hadn't eroded her sense of humor.

"Completely," Sasha said. "I think you'll appreciate my Muppet Aesthetic. I prefer all non-shedding dogs to have cuddle quality."

"That's why I called you. Someone mentioned this Muppet Aesthetic. I'm not sure she meant it to be a compliment, but it struck exactly the right note for me."

"Isn't that always the way?" Sasha said. "You can't please everyone, but for some you're just right."

"I like your attitude, young lady," Mrs. Barber said. "It can be hard to make lemonade in this town but I see you're doing it."

"I love Dog Town lemonade," Sasha said. "Now where shall I perform my teddy bear magic?"

An hour later, Garnet came out of the downstairs bathroom prancing as only a poodle can. It had taken some serious combing and cutting, but she'd been friendly and cooperative, anticipating what Sasha needed before she knew herself. The dog even offered her paws one by one for trimming, and a splash of silver nail polish.

"Oh my, she's perfect," Mrs. Barber said, when the dog leaped into her lap. "Look at her gorgeous toes! And she's so soft!"

"Garnet's coat is extremely curly," Sasha said. "I'm sure it's hard to brush, so if you'd like me to drop by now and then to do it I wouldn't charge you. It will save work on my next formal visit." She caught herself. "Assuming you'll have me back."

"I most certainly will. But may I ask another favor? I'd like a photo to text to my nephew."

Sasha took Mrs. Barber's phone and snapped some good shots of Garnet sitting. "He's a poodle fan? So few men are. Although Mayor Bradshaw is raising their profile with his dog, Princess."

Mrs. Barber chuckled as she sent off the text. "Not at all. My nephew is a lovely boy, but I think he finds Garnet embarrassing. He doesn't like walking her."

Sasha laughed. "I figured."

"In every other way I couldn't ask for a better nephew, though. He moved back here to look out for me when I got sick, and he's not Dorset Hills' biggest fan."

"Why not? It's such an interesting town."

The old woman shook her head. "Girl trouble, perhaps. Years ago, someone broke his heart during a visit. Left a bad taste in his mouth, I guess."

"Well, the love of a good dog could cure that," Sasha said. "It's working for me. And poodles really are the smartest breed. My Tuni is a Welsh springer spaniel. She's a sweetheart, but she's born to run, not to think."

Mrs. Barber laughed. "Don't tell me... a man chose the breed."

"My ex, yes. No way would he consider a poodle—even when I told him I'd turn it into a teddy bear. He wanted a hunting dog, although he's never held a gun in his life."

"Men are so silly. My late husband always wanted a big smelly retriever. I loved that man but he was barely cold when I bought Garnet. My nephew jokes that he's turning in his grave over Garnet taking over his favorite chair. But this little girl is the light of my life, especially now that I'm practically housebound."

"She's a lovely dog, really. You've raised her well."

The old woman beamed. "She was that way from the start. Never gave me a moment's trouble. Take a look on the mantel and see her puppy pictures."

Sasha picked up one frame after the other, finally coming to a photo of a young man holding Garnet. His hair was nearly the same shade as the dog's. Although his face looked familiar, the only redhead she knew in Dorset Hills was Mike from the mayor's office.

"I feel like I've seen this man before," she told Mrs. Barber, "although I haven't been in town long."

"That's the nephew I mentioned," she said, beaming. "It was years ago, when Garnet was just a pup. He's shaved off all his hair now. Said he was tired of ginger jokes." She sighed. "The hair will grow back, but the tattoos break my heart."

"Oh." Sasha put the frame on the shelf as if it had become hot enough to burn her fingers. "I don't understand tattoos myself. As for red hair, maybe he should just focus on how rare it is. Only two percent of the population has it. I was a hairstylist in my former life, and I met very few people with that gorgeous shade of auburn."

"I'll tell him you said so," she said.

"I wouldn't," she said. "No one listens to hairstylists or dog groomers."

"Now, now, Sasha, you're being too hard on yourself. You're a clever girl and I just know you're going to do well in Dorset Hills. Give it time, please. Doors can be slow to open around here."

"And sometimes they slam on your fingers when they do."

"True. I've always lived here, and loved it, but I do see it through new eyes since my nephew moved back. Sometimes I worry the town is losing its heart, but I really think it's just a few bad eggs with loud voices. Underneath, we're all dog-lovers."

"I hope you're right. I thought I'd landed in heaven when I got here, but it's been a tough year."

"Have faith. A true love of dogs always stands the test, and I can see you have it."

"That I do."

There was a steady click of nails over hardwood and

then a huff-huff-snort. Suddenly a canine bowling ball picked up speed and rolled into Sasha's knees hard. She grabbed the back of an upholstered chair. Instead of supporting her, it tipped over and she tumbled to the floor.

Grover walked around it and started licking her face.

"Grover!" Mrs. Barber said. "Get off her. Off! Griffin, help! Grover's got the groomer pinned under a chair."

"It's okay," Sasha said. "Don't worry, I'm fine."

Thumping footsteps followed and the soft skid of socks across polished floors.

Griffin stared down at her as he moved the chair. "What are you doing here?"

She could barely see him as she fended Grover off with her one free hand. "Would you mind? I'm always glad to see Grover, but I do wish he'd let me stay on my feet."

"You've met!" Mrs. Barber said. "Now you can tell Griffin the statistics about redheads."

"Don't bother," he said, grinning. "I already know I'm unique."

"I have to get going, anyway." She accepted his hand and scrambled to her feet. When she let go, it felt like he held on just a second too long. Or was that her? Either way, her palm tingled in an odd way and the little warning bell in her head pinged.

"Stay for tea," Mrs. Barber said. "I think you two would like each other. You have so much in common."

"Well, we don't agree on poodles," Sasha said. "For starters."

"What normal red-blooded man admits to liking poodles?" he asked, stooping to pick up Garnet, who was dancing in circles in front of him on her hind legs like a circus performer.

"The mayor?" Sasha asked, tying back her hair.

He rolled his eyes. "He's normal?"

Still in her chair, Mrs. Barber had missed the cues. "Griffin loves all animals," she said. "And he's a talented carpenter."

Examining Garnet's paws, he said, "Someone's hitting the polish again."

"I love it," his aunt said. "Don't be so negative, Griffin. There's nothing wrong with catering to dogs and dog-lovers. In fact, it's the only thing that makes sense in this silly town."

"Nothing makes sense in this town."

"Embrace the silliness, and your gorgeous doghouses will be a hit."

He shuddered. "I thought I could but I feel like a sell-out. I'd rather work in construction."

"But you're an artist, honey," she said. "Few have your gift."

Sasha agreed but wouldn't say so. The doghouses she saw in his yard were unique and appealing. They were art, and the type of thing that would catch on like wildfire in Dorset Hills if he actually opened his gate.

"Thank you, Aunt Helen," he said, letting Garnet snuggle under his chin. "I appreciate your support, you know that."

"Look at them," Mrs. Barber said. "He adores this dog, and then gets himself a bruiser he can't even pick up."

"I love how you aligned your names... Griffin and Grover," Sasha said. "It's adorable."

Griffin winced and gestured to his aunt. "She named him."

"I did," his aunt said, laughing. "He just looked like a Grover. Once I got it into my head I couldn't stop."

Grover was loitering at Sasha's feet happily as she gathered her equipment. "He's quite a character," she said.

"I do worry about his respiratory problems," Mrs. Barber said. "Griffin's afraid to let him go under an anesthetic in case—"

"Aunt Helen. Please."

"Well, fine. But he's my great-nephew and I care about him."

When Grover figured out Sasha was leaving, he wrapped his paws around her shin. Griffin tried to unlock the hold, but the dog was like a professional wrestler.

"Grover, let Sasha go," Mrs. Barber said. "And Griffin, you stop laughing right now. It's not funny."

"I know, I'm sorry," Griffin said. "Let me help."

"No worries, I'm good," Sasha said. "A groomer has to develop some muscle."

And a very thick skin, apparently. Sasha dragged the dog with her for a couple of yards, adding 60-plus pounds to her already heavy load. Her exit was slow and extremely undignified until she remembered the liver treats in her pocket. Scattering them, she waited for Grover to let go and snuffle off. Then she picked up her grooming table in the front hall and hoofed it.

CHAPTER NINETEEN

The wedding had sounded wonderfully romantic when the bride called last minute, and Sasha couldn't resist the opportunity to make new contacts. How hard could it be to spend three hours attending to a pair of young huskies named Yuri and Lara? She had little knowledge of the breed, but they always seemed reserved and sedate.

She packed her brushes and grooming lotions carefully, and gave less thought to her own appearance. It was enough to be presentable when she was just a hired hand. A little black dress with some room to move would suffice, along with a nice pair of heels and a simple up-do to keep her hair out of the way. Her favorite coat had been ripped in the dog rescue, leaving only her puffy parka and a light fall coat. She chose the black fall coat as it suited the occasion better.

The Renegade Inn, an old mansion on the outskirts of town, hosted dozens of weddings each year. In the summer, the grounds were stunning and more than made up for the slightly scruffy look of the building itself. Now, surrounded by lumpy, snow covered mounds and bare trees, the inn looked its age.

Sasha debated wearing her boots but the parking lot was clear and salted, and her hands were full. It was easy enough to pick her way around the puddles and run up sandstone stairs covered in dingy red carpet.

"Oh good, you're here," the wedding planner said, grabbing her elbow as she came in. "The photographer's almost ready." The woman looked down. "Is that what you're wearing?"

"What's wrong with this?" She glanced around and her outfit looked in keeping with the rest of the guests.

The planner blinked a couple of times and then tapped her tablet. "No time to second guess. You've only got 10 minutes to prep the dogs. They're in the back porch, waiting."

Lying in wait, was a more accurate description. Lara, the blue-eyed beauty, jumped on Sasha, hooking her claws into the lace at her waist. "Off," she said, unhooking the claws, one by one. Meanwhile Yuri stared warily with one blue eye; his brown eye looked friendlier. Both dogs started pacing, clearly anxious over being shoved out of the way in a strange place. She couldn't blame them. The wide back windows looked out over a barren landscape, where gardens blended into a golf course that stretched on forever.

Setting her black bag on a table, she opened it and pulled out her brush. Lara darted away from her, and Yuri's hackles lifted slightly.

"Now, now, none of that," she said, undeterred. "I'm getting paid to make sure you look and smell good." She reached into her bag and pulled out a container full of dried, rolled cod skins. Few dogs could resist them, and happily, Yuri was no exception. His hackles settled and she was able to run the brush over him and smooth his coat with a shine lotion. Lara was less willing, and she let the dog jump on her just to manage finger combing.

Looking down, she gasped. Her black dress and coat were covered in long, silvery hair. Pulling a lint roller out of her bag, she set to work on her own grooming, but the lace locked onto the hair like spiderweb.

The door opened and the wedding planner stuck her head in. "Oh my," she said. "I'd button up your coat. Now, let's go. Everyone's dressed."

"Dressed?" Sasha trailed after her with the dogs on a double leash. "What do you mean?"

The wedding party was walking through a side door, and she hurried after them. There must be a party room downstairs.

The door actually opened onto the outdoor patio. A narrow path had been shovelled across the stones, and then out across the snow-covered lawn to the gazebo.

"Oh no," Sasha said.

"Let's go," the planner said.

The bride and groom led the way, laughing and bantering with the guests. He was wearing a heavy gray wool coat and a big fur hat. She was wearing a trailing white cape trimmed with matching fur. As they arranged themselves outside the gazebo, it became a scene straight out of Dr. Zhivago.

"Seriously?" Sasha hissed at the event planner. "No one thought to mention it was an outdoor shoot?"

"The dogs will only be in a few shots," the planner called over her shoulder.

Sasha had fallen behind. The dogs were pulling hard together on the double leash and the path was slippery from so many footsteps. She slammed the spike of her heel down with each step to get a bit of traction.

"Yuri! Lara!" the bride caroled out. "Ready for your close-up?"

The dogs leapt forward, off the path, and started galloping across the lawn through nearly two feet of snow. Sasha only stayed on her feet for a few seconds, before toppling onto her side. Still holding the leash in her left hand, she managed to roll and the dogs dragged her the last 10 yards flat on her back.

Several groomsmen rushed to her aid. One took the leash, another helped her to her feet, and a third ran back for her bag, which sat like a black island in the snow. Yuri and Lara were leaping all over the happy couple. The bride screamed, but luckily the dogs were covered only in snow.

"Where's the groomer?" the bride called. "You were supposed to keep them leashed at all times."

"They pulled the girl over," her new husband said. "Her dress was up around her ears." He laughed and then stopped. "Not that I was looking."

"I was," his best man said, grinning. "And it wasn't."

"Too bad," the other groomsman said. He grinned at Sasha. "Just kidding."

Her face felt hot enough to melt all the snow. "Sorry," she said. "They're very strong."

"Never mind, all of you," the bride said. "It's *my* day and I won't have it ruined by dogs of either species." She handed the leashes to the event planner, who transferred them back to Sasha.

"Can someone get the groomer a real coat?" the best man asked. "She's freezing."

"I'm okay, really," Sasha said. "We won't be long."

The event planner pulled out her phone. "I'll get the staff to find something."

Sasha forced herself to stop shivering by focusing on

drying the dogs with a microfiber towel. It served her right for not dressing properly for a Dorset Hills winter, she figured, and she wasn't going to let a chill stop her from getting the job done well. Gigs like this one could generate word of mouth like nothing else. Hopefully she'd be seen as intrepid, if a little naïve.

Now that the dogs were near their owner they calmed down, and it wasn't hard to maneuver them into position for their shots. She even "set designed" a few, arranging the cape in a curved sweep while the dogs lounged beside it. The blonde bride looked icy and imperious and the groom dark and dashing. She had to admit that the photos would be breathtaking. She managed to take a couple of pictures with her phone before the leash was back in her hand.

"Take them to the front porch and someone will drive them home," the planner said. "Then you can leave." She ran her eyes over Sasha. "Send me the bill for dry cleaning."

The coat could at least be saved, she thought, taking it slow on the walk back. The dress was a goner.

They were just 15 yards from the inn when a large brown hare shot out of a bush. It hopped past them and disappeared around the side of the building. The dogs leapt as one and pulled as sled dogs were bred to do. Sasha held tight and bolted with them. She lost both shoes quickly, which actually made running easier. Around the side they went at a gallop. Her yelling seemed to spur them on. They followed the small footprints directly into a long, high hedge, still green and spiky. As the dogs disappeared into the wall of greenery, she had no choice but to let go.

Cursing, she shoved her arms through the bushes and forced her way through. By then the dogs were out of sight. She followed their trail of broken snow and ended up on her butt once more. Finally, shouts made her turn.

Four men in suit jackets came through the bushes to help. Looking up, she saw dozens of faces pressed to the glass, and several people tapping and pointing west.

"They went that way," she said, raising one icy hand. It wobbled as her body shuddered with cold.

"We've got it," one man said, running off with two others.

The fourth man took her arm. "They'll find the dogs and bring them back. Come inside."

She scrambled to her feet, tears filling her eyes. "Griffin? What are you doing here?"

"Less talk, more walk," he said, practically carrying her. Now that the leashes were officially out of her hands, she could feel how cold her feet were. More specifically, she could feel nothing but pins and needles where her feet used to be. They didn't work properly.

"I need to wait for the dogs. It's my job." She grabbed the rusty brass railing to stop him from dragging her up the stairs.

"You don't lose your feet for wedding photos," he said. "Now, walk or be carried? How do you want to make your entrance?"

She walked up the stairs with his help. Inside, he led her to the kitchen, and found her a chair in the corner. After a short discussion with the kitchen staff, he came back with a blanket and then carried over a large basin of steaming water.

"Not yet, not yet," he said, kneeling beside her as she tried to slip her bare feet into the water. Her stockings had shredded, leaving only reddened toes. At least they weren't white from frostbite. "You'll live to dance again. Though probably not tonight."

"I lost the bride's dogs. My name will be mud."

"They're huskies. Huskies run. Huskies pull. Huskies kill rabbits if they catch them."

"No! Please tell me they didn't—"

"They didn't," he said, testing the water. Then he took her feet by the ankles, and lifted them one by one into the basin.

She pulled them out again quickly. "Ow. Hot, hot."

"Just go slowly," he said.

"Griffin? What's going on?" Mrs. Barber pushed into the kitchen using a walker. Her face broke into a smile when she saw Sasha. "Oh my dear, I'm so sorry about what happened. Those dogs!"

"It's okay, Aunt Helen," Griffin said. "Please go back and sit down. I'll be right with you."

"Huskies!" she said. "The way they grabbed—"

"Aunt Helen! It's all fine now."

"What a mess," she finished. "You did your best, Sasha. Huskies are lovely dogs, but they're half wild. The bride would be better off with a nice pair of—"

"Poodles?" Sasha guessed. She was reviving enough to manage a smile.

"Exactly," Mrs. Barber said, turning her walker and leaving.

"Or bulldogs," Griffin said. "Grover can pull, but he can't run."

She laughed, suddenly very conscious of his hands on her bare ankles. Her dress was hitched too high and she pushed it down. Taking one hand out of the water, he plucked a few long dog hairs from her dress.

"Your suit," she said, just to dispel the awkward feeling that suddenly filled her. "This floor is dirty." Why was he being so nice to her all of a sudden? And why did his hand feel so much warmer than the hot water?

"It's okay." He kept his left hand on her ankles, making sure they were immersed. "Just a few more minutes."

One of the serving staff came in carrying a pair of sneakers, athletic socks, and a towel. Griffin set them on a chair and then lifted her feet out of the basin. He was about to start drying them when she said, "I got it. I'm okay now. Thank you."

He smiled up at her and it was a completely different smile from the smirk he usually wore. It was wide, and kind and— No.

She stopped that train of thought and redirected it. She was delusional after her experience. Even if she were looking for a relationship, Griffin wasn't her type. Aside from the bald head and tattoos, he had a big attitude and too little control over his dog. That might be the pot calling the kettle black, but she felt fine doing that. Even if he was taking very good care of her. Even if his hand on her knee felt heavy and warm and comforting. Even if— *No.* He was a bad risk.

"Listen, I've been thinking about Tuni," he said. "And while it's still highly unlikely that Grover could have... *you know...* it seems like they were alone together at the right time. So there's a chance. And if there's a chance, I really do want to do the right thing."

"Oh yeah? What *is* the right thing?" she asked.

"I don't know. This is all new to me. But whatever it is, I'll help."

"Can we not talk about this here? There are ears everywhere."

"That there are." He sat back on his heels and stared up at her. His eyes were a beautiful, translucent green—as rare as his red hair. And he seemed to ooze masculinity in a way her ex, Lawrence, never had. It was a bit unnerving, if she was honest. Maybe more than a bit.

"Well, well, look what the dogs dragged in," a familiar voice said.

Sasha glanced up and found Bartholomew Barnes leaning on his cane. "Hey Bart," she said, grinning. "Where's Puck?"

"Not invited," he said. "Although there are twenty other dogs here."

"I told you to let me groom him," she said. "He's being judged on his looks."

"And I told you that no one likes a bossy groomer, as I recall." Griffin snickered and Bart gestured with his cane. "Help her up, my boy. I'm without a date for this grand affair. Put your sneakers on and join me, young lady."

"That's a bad idea," she said, pulling on the athletic socks and then the shoes. "I'm sure the bride's upset with me over what happened."

"The bride is my niece," Bart said. "She has some strange ideas about dogs. I'll have a word with her about those huskies."

"Not today. It's her day."

"She probably wouldn't hear me with that silly cape over her head anyway," he said, nodding to Griffin as if to signify the official handoff. "Thank you, young man. Now, Sasha, the boys brought in your bag. I suggest you get your phone and take some photographs of all the dogs my niece considered better than Puck. We'll need them to build my case."

That job kept her from thinking too much about her footwear, or her botched job handling the huskies. Indeed, she managed to avoid the bride and groom completely for the next hour or so as Bart guided their stroll around the reception hall. He continued to suggest dogs and angles for shots, long after she was ready to go.

"Thank you, Bart. You're a real prince."

"An old prince," he said. "But there's room for plenty in the royal family of Dog Town."

CHAPTER TWENTY

Leo's ears came forward as much as a beagle's floppy flaps could. His muzzle sat in the crook of Remi's arm and his eyes stayed on Sasha's face, as if trying to pick up clues with his eyes, nose and ears and then transmit them to his owner through touch. Sasha hoped she'd have that kind of bond with Tuni some day. Leo and Remi were three years ahead of her.

"He washed your feet." It was a statement because Remi had already used up her question marks. "In a basin. Kneeling at your side."

"You're giving it religious overtones that really don't suit the occasion." Sasha leaned on the smooth counter and smiled down at Remi, who was in her usual place on the old oak pew. It seemed like she spent more time at the salon now than she did at the hospital foundation. The steady stream of dogs coming in to collect their free nail trims was irresistible. "He just felt bad for me about everything."

"I think maybe he feels more than that. Just my guess."

"You're reading more into it than there is."

"Okay." She didn't sound convinced. "But he still doesn't think Grover's the daddy."

Sasha shook her head. "I can understand that. Grover's a lovable cartoon of a dog—when he isn't humping mine. But to me the evidence is clear: Tuni got into his yard, and Grover helped make it happen. There was probable cause and no alibi."

"But there's no way of knowing until the pups arrive."

"Exactly. If they're snorty little piglets, we'll have our answer."

"And Griffin wants to do the right thing." Another statement. "He'll help out. Even without proof."

"So he said." Her tone was skeptical. "People say things they don't mean all the time, and never follow through."

Leo lifted his head, eyes alert. It was as if he sniffed a secret. Sasha straightened her shoulders. She might be able to fool Remi, but Leo was a different matter.

Picking up on some clue, Remi said, "Who exactly are we talking about now?"

The bells rang, and Sasha heaved a grateful sigh as Carole came in with her walker. Remi set Leo down and went to help.

"Good morning, girls," Carole said. "What's the scuttlebutt? It looks like you were knee-deep in Dog Town scandals. Don't stop on my account. Please."

Remi laughed as she took Carole's coat. "I wish I knew more about Dog Town's seedy underbelly. If you've got the dirt, do share."

Carole pushed up to the counter. She was already walking so much better. Sometimes it looked like she didn't need the walker anymore, but then she'd clutch it again. It would probably take time to feel stable again.

"I was always up to date when I was cutting hair," she

said. "The scissors are like a magic wand for magnetizing gossip."

"Agreed," Sasha said. "I always knew who was breaking up or making up or going broke. Sometimes before they did."

"Or pregnant," Carole said.

Sasha turned to stare at her, but Carole had grabbed a cloth and started dusting the glass shelves beside the counter.

"Pregnant?" Remi's question marks were back. "How so?"

"Hair quality," Carole said, reaching up to straighten the stuffed spaniel on the top shelf. "Your hair goes funny when those hormones kick in. A stylist is as good as a pregnancy test."

"Good to know," Remi said, laughing.

"Planning on using my skills?" Carole asked. "You've been with that Iverson boy a while now."

"Four months!" Remi's face flamed, and she turned to grab her coat off the pew.

"Four months plus twelve years," Carole said. "In high school, my daughter used to say, 'Remi Malone's already got a boyfriend, why can't I?'"

"Well, we're new again," Remi said, leaning to pick up Leo. "No hair assessments required anytime soon."

Her hasty exit was blocked by a man coming into the salon. She stepped sideways, and he stepped the same way. She stepped back and he did the same. Finally she backed up and he offered his hand. "Hello. I'm Rodney Crump."

"Remi Malone." She smiled, but it faltered when Leo reared back in her arms.

"Hello, ladies," he said, pleasantly. "I was in the neighborhood returning some Christmas gifts. Just thought I'd say hello."

Remi backed away from the door and looked at Sasha, expecting to be introduced. Carole glanced up from the shelves and then went back to her dusting.

"Remi, Carole, this is Mr. Crump," Sasha said. "He works for the Canine Corrections Department."

"The CCD?" Remi asked. "Is this visit business or social?"

"Social, of course," he said. His rubbery features coalesced into a pleasant smile, or something that passed for one. "I enjoyed my chat with Sasha last week and just wanted to say hello. I see you've taken my advice to heart."

"Advice? What advice?" Remi's voice had a sharp edge that was enough to make Leo shift anxiously.

Rodney Crump gestured to Sasha to fill in the blanks for the others.

"He suggested I hire help," she told Remi. "He said it was risky leaving the storefront empty while I was in the back with a dog, and risky leaving a dog at the back if I came to the front."

"So that's why you hired me," Carole said, smiling. "I thought it was for my charm and connections."

"Those were an added bonus," Sasha said. "What can I do for you today, Officer Crump?"

"Call me Rod," he said, offering his hand to Carole, who shook it warmly, and then Remi, who gave it a limp pump with her right hand as she groped in her pocket with her left.

"I'll make coffee," Carole said. "Why don't you have a seat while I earn my pay?"

"I have a dog coming in a few minutes," Sasha said. "No time for chitchat."

"I'd love a coffee, thank you," he said. "I hate returning gifts, don't you? There was hardly a thing I could keep this year."

"That's a shame," Sasha said. "I'm sure people tried very hard to find the right thing. It's hard to know the right thing sometimes."

"So true," Remi said, looking up from her phone. "Other times you know exactly what to do."

She sat on the pew, looked at Sasha and patted the space beside her. Before Sasha could get there, Rodney Crump sat down. Then he patted the bench beside him for Sasha. Soon they were lined up in a row. Remi looked uneasy as she got Leo settled in her lap. Rodney looked delighted. And Sasha's face clenched with worry. Why was he here again? What did he want?

Carole came out with three half-filled mugs of coffee rattling on the tray of her walker.

After a few minutes of awkward silence, the doorbells rang and a cold wind blew in. In the open doorway stood Cori, with Bridget and Duff behind her. "Hi. We were in the neighborhood," she said.

Officer Crump sat back and crossed his arms. The movement suggested there was no need for introductions, but Sasha made them anyway.

"Close the door, you're letting winter in," Officer Crump said.

"There's no room for all of us," Cori said. "I figured you were leaving."

"I just got my coffee," he said, holding up a mug. "I'm happy to chat for a bit."

"Officer Rod is returning Christmas gifts today," Remi said. "He's hard to buy for."

"Easy," Cori said. "Binoculars. Those teeny-tiny ones so people won't even know you're spying."

He laughed. "Ms. Hogan, you have the wrong idea about me."

"Let's check. I have the idea that you're here scaring Sasha with silly threats you've concocted. Am I right?"

"Not at all." His tone was smooth and playful. He clearly relished sparring with Cori. "The CCD isn't about giving people a hard time. We're here to help people like Sasha succeed."

Duff pushed back her hood and spoke for the first time. "That's wonderful. How are you helping Sasha today?"

"Just checking in to make sure business is going okay. A friendly call."

Bridget made a face. "In other words, no help at all. The CCD was equally helpful to me around the time of my pageant."

Cori made a sound of disgust. "Is it any wonder Santa got your gifts all wrong, Rod? You're on the naughty list."

"Now Cori," Duff said. "Let's take Mr. Crump's words at face value. Everything changes, including the CCD. So how exactly can you help Sasha make a success of her business?"

"By making sure she doesn't cross any lines," he said. "When you're new in town, it's hard to know who's on the right side, isn't it?"

"I've never been new," Cori said. "Born and raised here. So I know exactly where I stand at all times."

"Me too," Remi said.

"I'm not a lifer, but I still know right from wrong," Duff said.

"I don't feel confused at all," Bridget said.

"Doesn't mean you aren't," he said.

Cori came over and picked up the mug he'd set on the pew between Sasha and himself. "Coffee's cold, Officer Rod. I think the party's over."

"I can take a hint," he said, laughing as he got to his feet.

"Wonderful," Cori said. "Because I'm a master of subtlety. Everyone says so."

The laughter from the women was louder than the doorbells when he left.

CHAPTER TWENTY-ONE

Sasha was bundled in down, wool and fleece and wearing heavy winter boots. "Wow, I will never be cold again," she whispered.

"What's that?" Remi asked, turning back. She'd left Leo at home for this expedition to the parking lot of the old trail system.

"Nothing." Sasha hadn't asked where they were going. Cori was furious that she'd kept Officer Crump's first visit a secret and it was as if Sasha had become invisible.

The trail they were on was nearly invisible, too. It was probably dangerous to be out here on a blustery grey winter day. She was surprised the parking lot was even plowed.

"She won't come," Cori said to no one in particular. She seemed to be mad at everyone.

Bridget and Duff exchanged glances over Cori's head. They probably did that a lot. It was convenient that the scrappy master trainer was so tiny.

"She'll come," Bridget said. "She owes me."

"But then you'll owe her," Cori said.

"I'm okay with that," Bridget said. "I always owe

someone something and someone always owes me. It's the Dog Town underground currency system."

"I can't stand owing anything," Cori muttered, kicking a branch out of the way. She almost slipped and two hands came out and steadied her. She shrugged them off immediately. "Especially to her. Traitor."

"She's not a traitor," Bridget said. "We know her well. Or we used to before she became a—"

"Sneaky no-good traitor."

"People don't change that much overnight. She had her reasons for what she did. Maybe she'll tell us what they are today."

"If you're not hostile," Duff said, pulling her scarf down to speak. "If you can keep a muzzle on it."

Cori pushed her hat back to glare at Duff. "When did you become full-fledged Mafia? Did the vote happen when I was away?"

"Am I full-fledged?" Duff said. "*Just when I thought I was out... they pull me back in.*"

She did her best Pacino impression and Remi and Sasha laughed.

"I'm only half joking," Duff called back to them. "You ladies be careful not to get pulled into the criminal life."

"That ship probably sailed when I lassoed that rescue dog," Sasha said.

"Don't mention that today," Duff said. "Be very careful about what you say."

"It can and will be used against you," Cori said. "By the traitor. I can't believe you told her where we meet, Bridget. You've broken a sacred code."

"It had to be safe for her, too, Cori. She can't help if she's seen with us." She gestured to the bronze statue ahead of them. "I'd hate to give up this spot, but we can find another."

The eight-foot statue was a chow chow with a white crown that hadn't melted since the last storm. Bridget patted the big dog like an old pal.

The crunch of boots on snow made them turn. A woman trudged toward them up the trail. She pulled her scarf from her face and smiled. Her eyes were warm and brown, and the hair spilling out from under her hat was also dark. She looked friendly and kind… not like a traitor at all.

Cori perched on the platform at the bottom of the chow chow and crossed her arms. She angled her legs sideways so that she didn't have to look at the traitor, but could still see everything that happened.

"She's still mad?" the woman asked Bridget.

Bridget nodded. "Still mad. Can you blame her, Kinney? You changed sides."

Kinney's smile faded, but only a bit. "Not from my perspective. I changed *jobs*. More specifically, I got a job after being unemployed and broke."

"Better broke than a traitor," Cori mumbled.

Duff gave her a poke with her mitten. "Muzzle it."

"I needed a job, Cori," Kinney said. "And believe it or not, I thought I might do some good on the CCD. I loved working with you guys, but the tide was turning with this new political regime and I thought I might have more influence inside."

"How's that been working out so far?" Cori asked. "The judge just got fired and that idiot Cliff Whorley's heading up dog court. I'd say politics are winning."

"It's a long game," Kinney said. "I'm in it to win it."

Cori turned to face her. "That's where we disagree. I don't think it's a game at all."

"Okay, okay." Bridget raised both mittens. "We can hash this out another day, ideally somewhere warm. Sasha Wildwood, meet Kinney Butterfield. She used to work closely with us, but joined the Canine Corrections Department recently as a dog cop."

Kinney shook Sasha's hand and smiled. "I'm still one of the good guys."

"How about Officer Rodney Crump?" Sasha asked. "Is he also a good guy?"

"I don't know him well," she said staring up at the chow chow. "But I doubt we'll hang out much."

"In other words, no," Sasha said. "Why would he want me out of business?"

"It's not personal," Kinney said. "There's pressure within the CCD—the government at large really—to be seen as taking control of the dog problem."

"What dog problem?"

"More like a mayoral problem," Cori said.

Kinney ignored Cori. "Sasha, you're new to the machinations in Dorset Hills. All I can say is that City Council is a little touchy right now. About a lot of things... dating back to Thanksgiving, actually."

"My pageant didn't cause problems," Bridget said. "It shone light on them."

"A lot of lights. From New York City cameras. The mayor will be in a panic until that TV feature airs."

"It's going to make Dog Town look good," Bridget said. "The producer promised me that."

"Then things will settle down," Kinney said. "In the meantime, it's volatile and we're being pressed to—"

"Do the wrong thing," Cori said. "Send bad dogs out of Dog Town. Fire judges who try to be reasonable."

"Marti Forrester is a good person," Kinney said. "She

hired me, you know. Cliff didn't want me. He really didn't want me."

Finally, Cori's shoulders relaxed and she stood up. "Really? He hates you?"

"Pretty much, yeah. Does that make you feel better?"

Cori almost smiled. "Actually, yeah. He must be worried you haven't been fully inculcated by the CCD brainwashers."

"He's right to worry," Kinney said. "My mind is still my own. This job isn't easy, you know, and I often wish I'd never applied. But I'm making the best of it."

Bridget stepped forward. "Can you find out what this Crump guy has on Sasha? If we know, we can fix it. She's risked her life savings to set up this salon, and she's also one of the good guys. I think you know you can trust me on that."

Kinney nodded. "I do trust you. But I'm actually not privy to why Rod's targeting The Model Dog, if he is at all."

"He is," Bridget said. "It was quite clear that he was there to intimidate her. It bordered on harassment."

"She didn't tell us about his first visit," Cori said, without looking at Sasha.

"Probably because she didn't want to get you into trouble," Kinney said. "Am I right?"

Sasha nodded. "I don't want anyone to get into trouble on my account. Including you. All I wanted to do was settle into this town and contribute. But everything's more complicated than I expected."

"It is," Kinney agreed. "I know you had a really hard time after you moved here. I'm sorry about that."

"Hard time?" Cori asked. "What else don't we know?"

"It's personal," Sasha said. "Nothing the CCD should want to know."

"It's my job to know things," Kinney said, shrugging. "It helps paint a full picture."

"She was always a great sleuth," Duff said. "It helped us before, and hopefully it will help us again."

"I can't risk my job," Kinney said. "I have vet bills after Kali passed."

Cori and Bridget looked down and scuffed their boots in the snow, and Duff patted Kinney's sleeve. Everyone knew the pain of losing a pet, and acknowledging it seemed to shift the mood. The sun actually broke through the clouds and glinted off the great chow.

"What if we could help you score points in your job while you help protect an innocent and upstanding groomer?" Duff said. "You make whatever Rod's got on Sasha go away and we'll give you a bone to take to Cliff."

"I doubt you know much I don't already know," Kinney said. "No offence."

"Offence taken," Cori said. "I know plenty you don't know. Contrary to popular opinion, I keep quiet on some things until the time is right."

"What have you got?" Kinney said.

"Your word first," Duff said. "No offence."

"I'm still the same person, Duff," Kinney said. "But if you need to hear it out loud, you have my word."

"A puppy mill," Duff said. "Something to distract Cliff and get some press while you make this go away."

"I've got a list of puppy mills as long as the hills system," Kinney said. "Most of them are out of our jurisdiction."

"One of them isn't," Bridget said. "A big one. We wanted to take care of it ourselves, so that we could place the dogs in good homes. If we give it to you, who knows what will happen?"

"It's my job to protect animals." Kinney's voice got sharp. "Honestly, Bee, you know I wouldn't harm a dog."

"I know *you* wouldn't," Bridget said. "It's your colleagues I worry about. So here's how it will go: you suss out the Sasha problem and we tell you where the puppy mill is. You extract the dogs and let us know where you hold them. We place them properly. Deal?"

"Deal." Kinney offered her mitten and Bridget shook it. Cori made retching sounds from the foot of the chow chow. "Deal with the devil," she said.

"The devil you know is better than the devil you don't," Kinney said, starting back down the trail. "And I miss you too, folks."

CHAPTER TWENTY-TWO

Hiring Carole had turned out to be a wise decision. No matter what nefarious plans the CCD might have, business continued to boom at The Model Dog and it was tough to juggle sometimes. The free peticures started to pay off as owners followed up with full grooming appointments. On top of everything else, she continued to get private primping gigs, like weddings, christenings, family portraits and even a funeral. Her little black bag wasn't big enough for the costumes she needed. Those had gone over so well that she had a local seamstress creating a custom line. Everyone wanted something original for photos, so she got formal dog frocks in various styles and colors, vests for the boys, and all sorts of accessories. Some she kept for private clients, but others she let Carole display in the salon and people started coming in just to buy canine clothes. Of course, Tuni modelled something cute every day. The designer had a special line that fastened over the privates, which kept the outfits in place no matter how rough the play. You just had to remember to unfasten for potty breaks.

Sasha had Mrs. Gunner and Rory to thank for that great idea.

"Leave Tuni with me," Carole said, as she hooked up the dog's leash. "You can't take her to this shoot, can you?"

"I'll drop her off at home. I find she gets overstimulated from a full day on the job."

In fact, she didn't like Tuni to be out of her sight for even a moment. Even in her green satin gown today, she was looking a little... well, stout. If Carole decided to investigate further, she'd find the dog was carrying a full load.

A full load of *what* still wasn't clear. Last week's ultrasound had been inconclusive. Dr. Benson predicted six or seven puppies, tops, and said there was "nothing exceptional" about them. On the bright side, that eased Sasha's anxiety about leaving her with the Doggie Doula. Average puppies hopefully made for an easy entrance into the world.

Tuni would be heading off to the home for unwed mothers in just a few days, and Sasha had become clingy. Most nights, they crashed on the couch together exhausted, with Tuni's head on her chest. The dog had never been more affectionate and she hoped that wouldn't change in their two months apart.

"What's wrong?" Carole asked. "You look sad, and yet everything is coming up roses for you."

"I wouldn't say roses." She didn't want to be rubbing anything in Carole's face given that her former shop was the foundation of her success. Besides, the roses in her life had some pretty sharp thorns. "I've got that CCD guy to worry about, for starters."

"Rod Crump?" She rolled her eyes. "He's just your typical wannabe cop, using his power for the wrong things. I've seen him coming out of Crackers and The Lucky Dog

Barkery a few times. He said he doesn't have a dog himself, so I bet he's giving lots of people a hard time. I really wouldn't worry about him, Sasha."

"That makes me feel a little better, although I'm sorry for the other people he's scaring."

"Nothing to be scared about." Carole used one hand to shove the rack of doggie dresses to the window. When things were slow, she put it there because few women could pass glittering gowns without coming in to take a look. Once she had them in the shop, she chatted them up, passed out cards and coffee, and generally worked her charm. She was definitely earning her wage.

"Thanks, Carole," Sasha said. "I really appreciate all you do here. Hiring you was my best decision since opening the salon."

"How sweet of you to say so when I practically forced myself on you," Carole said. "I'd work here for free if you must know. The money's a bonus."

"That kind of talk is only going to get you more hours," Sasha said, grinning.

"There's that smile," Carole said. "Keep it turned on and I bet you come home with two more gigs lined up."

"I'm too tired for more," Sasha said. "But with my vet bills, I wouldn't say no."

"Let me look around and see where we could make some savings." Carole started dusting the glass shelves, like she did every single day. "I can squeeze a nickel till it squeaks, you know. I had some very lean times here, especially toward the end."

"Don't you worry. I've got it all covered. A couple more gigs like this one and I'll be in the clear."

Sasha waved as she trudged over the icy sidewalk to the car. As usual, she caught the ever-migrating corner of the ice patch and nearly went down. Carole called the city every day about it, but nothing changed. It would take spring to fix the problem. With Valentine's Day only a week away, a thaw almost seemed possible now.

Romance was certainly in the air when she joined the Trent family for their daughter's engagement photos. Like most Dorset Hills brides, Amy Trent insisted that the family dogs be part of the shoot, and luckily both dogs were goldendoodles. Sasha had done the full groom the day before in the salon and they looked spectacular—like glorious lions that should flank a grand entrance. Their look had inspired the photographer to do the shoot at the St. Elgin Museum, which was also named after the town's founding family. The grand marble staircase in the foyer was the perfect backdrop, and the bride had chosen a pretty blue dress reminiscent of Marilyn Monroe. It was exactly the type of dress Sasha would choose, if she ever become engaged again. Not that she would. The first engagement had been an unmitigated disaster from the word, "Yes."

The shoot went off without a hitch. The dogs submitted to a good brushing and behaved impeccably, posing again and again. She stood behind the photographer, making kissing noises and crackling cod skins treats. The dogs were bright-eyed and more focussed than the humans.

At the end, she gave out some business cards and then strolled around the museum to avoid the sudden small snow squall that had whirled up during the session. Half an hour was more than enough to see all the exhibits. The building had been the manor home of a Dorset Hills founding family, and descendants had left it in the care of the City. The newer section was filled with dog paraphernalia, including a replica of the city that looked similar to the one in the Small Wonders Boutique Christmas display, only without the charm.

Sasha was staring at a breed chart that covered an entire wall when she heard heavy footsteps behind her. A man in City coveralls with the Labrador retriever coat of arms on the back set a ladder against a wall and started climbing. Something looked familiar, and it wasn't his butt. Coveralls didn't do anyone justice. A hammer dangled from his left hand, and above the wrist was a tattoo of an English bulldog.

"Hey," she said, looking up at Griffin.

He grabbed the oak frame of the doorway beside the ladder. "Never startle a man on a ladder," he said.

"I figured you saw me. I'm the only one left in the place."

"Head in the clouds," he said, climbing down. "What are you doing here?"

"Engagement shoot," she said. "Happily, no one dragged me around like a dogsled."

His face twitched and she knew he was fighting a smile. "I hope you're okay."

"You can laugh. I certainly did, once I thawed out. The dress is ruined, of course."

"It was a nice dress. But you'd look better in blue," he said. "Like that girl on the stairs."

Heat flared in her cheeks. "I'll keep that in mind. As for clothing choices... care to explain the coveralls? You didn't mention working for the city."

"It's a contract," he said. "Just started this week."

"I didn't peg you as a municipal employee."

He crossed his arms, and his sleeves slid up to reveal more tattoos. "Why is that? You think bald, tattooed guys don't want steady work?"

"I didn't think you'd like being told what to do by Dorset Hills leadership. That's all."

"Well, you're right about that," he admitted. "But I can suck it up as well as the next guy when there's money at stake. I'm on a mission to pay my aunt back what I borrowed to get set up as a carpenter. Then, once she's back on track, I can move out of this stupid town again."

"Now there's the attitude I expected."

He grinned, and it changed his face from forbidding to playful. "I wouldn't want to disappoint. I know you like things to go a certain way."

She moved over to the replica of the city and he followed. "You don't really know me," she said, searching among the little dog models for a spaniel. When she found one, she placed it in front of her shop on Main Street. "All you know is a worried groomer who's about to be a grandma."

"A grandma! So soon." He hunted around for a suitable model, and came up with a French bulldog. He set it beside the spaniel. "I must say you're the hottest grandma I've met in Dorset Hills."

"Thank you. I think." She picked up the spaniel and held it on the palm of her hand. "You won't talk about her, right? It would be bad news for the city to find out."

"Of course not. I may take the City's money but I don't need them poking around in my private affairs."

She tapped the roof of the CCD building in the city replica. "These folks have been sniffing around The Model Dog."

"Why? If I know you, you dotted every 'i' with a perfect little heart."

"I thought I did, but some guy has been giving me vague warnings. If they have something on me, they're not saying."

Now Griffin picked up the little spaniel. "Has this guy been eyeing her?"

She shook her head. "Not at all. And she's hard to ignore in her ballgowns and sweaters."

He rolled his eyes, and picked up the French bulldog. "I got a letter from the same people asking for proof of neuter. The new bylaw will take time to enforce, so I figure I might be gone before they do. But maybe they'll give me a hard time since I work for the city."

She took the French bulldog out of his hand and examined it. "I love scrunched up faces, I really do. I just don't want to see that on my grandkids."

Griffin leaned in a little closer. "Can you maybe not talk about being a dog grandma? I feel like it's one short jump to calling me granddad."

"Understood." She picked up the CCD building with both hands and deliberately moved it into Lake Longmuir.

Griffin snickered at that. Still holding the spaniel, he said, "How are you going to handle her situation with this dog cop hanging around? Can I help?"

She took the spaniel from his hand, stepped away, and placed it in Milverton. "She's going on vacation soon. I've got it covered."

"Let me come with you," he said, moving towards her. "The driving is terrible there this time of year. I have a big truck."

"I bet you say that to all the girls," she said.

"Only the ones I really want to impress. But I have the feeling it wouldn't work on someone like you."

"I'm not much for trucks," she said. "What impresses someone like me is a nice head of hair. And I know you're hiding one."

He swept off his City cap and bent over to reveal a fine

reddish stubble. He was growing his hair out... for her? The very idea caused her heart to flutter.

"Go for it," he said. "I know you want to."

She ran a finger lightly across his scalp, smiling at the prickly feeling. "Straight or curly?"

"It'll be a surprise," he said. "To both of us."

He lifted his head and his eyes were just inches from hers. Her heart twirled like Tuni in the dog park and did a little play pose.

"You can drive us," she said. "We're going on Saturday."

"It's a date then," he said. "Wear boots and a good coat. It's best to be prepared for anything around here."

"Good advice," she said, backing away. "Bye grandpa."

CHAPTER TWENTY-THREE

The Elgin Theater was about as glamorous as it got in Dorset Hills. The City had dreamed big when it teamed up with the founding family to build it a decade earlier. The magazine article that ultimately transformed Dorset Hills into Dog Town had been published around that time and civic leaders sensed the tide was turning. The Elgin Theater became a symbol: build it and they will come. The past couple of years had brought some decent theater troupes and popular musicians to the Elgin, which seated 1,800 at full capacity. The red carpet and plush seats were still fresh and welcoming for the very good reason that dogs weren't permitted. That the City had temporarily opened the venue to canine citizens spoke to its ambitions for the Valentine's Day gala.

The place smelled like promise, Sasha thought, as she walked down the aisle toward the stage on the morning of Saturday February 8th. That was exactly what Valentine's *should* smell like: hope and potential. Afterward, it would smell like reality, Dog Town style, and that was okay, too. She loved that the faint smell of dog clung to every public building in Dorset Hills. That was how you knew you were someplace special. They'd kept the Elgin too nice for too long. It was time to make it all it could be as a city hub.

The centre aisle was blocked by a temporary runway. The contestants would parade out for inspection, and the audience would use electronic devices to cast their vote for the most compelling owner-and-dog duo of each gender. The winners would get to enjoy the prize, which had expanded from a nice dinner to a full day of entertainment and spa treatments as donations continued to roll in. It could be amazing... or an absolute disaster. That was true of any first date, but this one would be filmed and televised.

"Sasha," Remi called from the stage. "We need to do a dry run. Can you hop onto the catwalk with Tuni?"

"Me?" She stared up at Remi. "I don't want to do the catwalk. You do it."

"I can't, I'm not a bachelorette," she said, grinning. "It would be bad luck."

"Very funny," Sasha said, walking up the stairs. "Well, I'm sure someone else can do that while I do some grunt work. I am the junior on the team, after all."

Mike laughed. "Remi has a point. I'm taken, too. Marsha?"

"Taken," she said, and the word rippled through the rest of the volunteers. How could it be that Sasha was the only single person in the house?

"The catwalk's all yours, Sasha," Mike said. "It's an important job. Only by imagining yourself in the role can you see how we can do better."

"Nice try, people. You're sticking it to the new kid."

She walked onto the stage and stood on the mark Remi had made with tape. Someone cued the music, and "Uptown Funk" blared out from the speakers. Coming up behind her, Remi eased the coat off her shoulders. Leaning close to her ear, she said, "It's a chance for you and Tuni to look like you haven't a care in the world. Shake it."

Shake it? Really. She was not going to put on a show for the old guard gossips of Dog Town. That very afternoon she had to part with her best friend, her sweet Tuni, because of people like them. She had done nothing terrible, except perhaps trust the wrong person to watch over her dog on the wrong day. It was a rookie mistake. How could someone who'd never owned a dog, let alone an intact one, know how serious the consequences could be of what seemed like a small error in judgement?

She lifted her chin and put her shoulders back. This was nothing but a blip on the radar of her life. She'd been through worse and survived. When Tuni got back, they'd start over and never look back. The Model Dog would become the premiere grooming salon in Dorset Hills, and then perhaps a chain. Why not dream big?

"Let's go, Tuni," she said. "Strut it, girl."

She stepped out with style, glad she'd worn boots with a nice heel and a flirty black skirt. The cashmere cardigan wasn't anything fancy, but it was blue and complimented her eyes. She wanted Griffin to notice that later, but not think she'd tried too hard. After all, today was all about Tuni. The dog was also in blue—a satin dress with frills at the waist. It wasn't flattering, but it did conceal a multitude of sins.

Down the catwalk they went, and when they reached the end, she gave a dramatic turn. Tuni trotted in a circle, her tail swishing back and forth. The dog loved to be front and center. Once Tuni was free of her precious cargo, Sasha would find ways to let the dog's light shine. Cori had suggested hunting trials to use her inbred talents, but agility training had more appeal.

The volunteers applauded, and Mike sent her down the catwalk again and again as they adjusted the lights and the sound.

"We need a bigger lip on that stage to protect the dogs on the turn," he said. "I booked a guy from City facilities but he didn't show. Luckily we have till Friday to get it fixed."

"Show's over, Tuni," Sasha said, leaving the catwalk. "Remi, I've gotta run."

Remi hugged her as if she were leaving on a space mission, rather than a drive to Milverton. "Be careful, okay?" Pulling away, her eyes filled with tears. "It'll all work out, my friend. I feel it in my bones."

"I know." Those two small words jammed like sawdust in her throat so she didn't force any more. Instead, she grabbed her coat, waved, and gave Tuni's leash a gentle tug. The dog looked up at her calmly, with a happy, trusting expression. They had come so far in just a month. Pregnancy really could work miracles, even if the circumstances weren't perfect.

TWO O'CLOCK CAME and went with no sign of Griffin. Sasha checked her phone again and again, as if a text could slip past her. At half past two, she texted him. At three, she swallowed hard and called. When the call went straight to voicemail, her throat clenched even tighter than it had earlier. How could he have forgotten? Worse, how could he ignore her texts and calls?

Well, there was no way she was driving by his house. If

he didn't want to come, she wouldn't twist his arm. She should have known better than to trust him. She *had* known better. Looking back, she saw the footbath was to blame. She'd lost perspective.

"Let's go, Tuni," she said, gathering the dog's bed, bowl, leash and complete wardrobe. She threw in some toys, as well. It was hard to imagine the new mama playing, but she dearly hoped Tuni wouldn't lose all her youthful ways just because of maternity. At least, not permanently.

Snow started before she'd passed the eight-foot Labrador retriever that marked the city border on the way to Milverton. It was going to be a slow, grim drive, but every moment with Tuni felt precious. The dog curled in the front seat in a baggy sweater, and rested her long sleek muzzle on Sasha's right leg. When there was a clear spot on the highway, she could stroke the dog's ears, and it slowed her pounding heart for just a second. Maybe she would mature into a therapy dog, after all.

Halfway through the drive, the phone rang. "Yes?" she said, picking up. It wasn't hard to sound cold. She was frozen from the inside out.

"Uh-oh," Remi said. Her voice echoed around the car and Tuni looked up. "What's wrong?"

"What's right would be easier to answer," Sasha said. "But for starters, Griffin stood me up."

"Stood you up? How can that be?"

"He didn't show, didn't answer his phone. Vanished off the planet." She gripped the steering wheel so tight her fingers ached. "That's what they do, when the going gets tough. Disappear. Ghost. Gone."

There was a long pause at the other end as Remi considered what to say. "I know how you feel, Sash," she said at last. "I really do, because I've been there. Tiller disappeared on me for a decade without explaining what happened. But it wasn't what I thought, remember? And everything came out right in the end. Better than it probably would have otherwise."

The breath she released was enough to cloud the windshield momentarily. "It didn't work that way for me. When Lawrence left, he really left. And never came back."

"You don't want him back, though... right?"

"I certainly do not. I could never trust him again." She reached for Tuni's head and the dog licked her hand. "It wasn't like Tiller. Lawrence left as soon as I got out of the hospital after a—an incident. In a new town, where I barely knew anyone. With the dog he chose, who wasn't in the best health herself. I was alone and sick and heartbroken. So, no, I don't want him back. Nothing he could do would make that right."

"I didn't know." Remi's voice was as full of sorrow as the dark clouds overhead were of snow. "You never said anything."

"No point," Sasha said. "It's behind me now. What's ahead is looking pretty bleak, too."

"Is that how Mim Gardiner knows you?"

She nodded, then realized Remi couldn't hear that. "Yes. But I'm fine now."

"Good. And Tuni will be fine, too. Come spring, everything will be like new. You have friends, remember?"

She nodded again. "I'm grateful for that. More than you know."

"Tonight, when you get back, I'll come over with Leo, okay?"

"I need Leo."

"And he needs to be needed. So we'll order some dinner and work on the script for the gala, okay?"

"Okay."

"You sound far away."

"I'm just fifteen minutes outside of Milverton now."

"I mean figuratively. My theory is that once Dog Town gets its teeth into you, the farther you go from the source, the weaker you get."

Sasha laughed at this. "Yep, it's in my blood, now. For better, for worse."

CHAPTER TWENTY-FOUR

It took a lot of makeup to cover the signs of tears, but showing up at The Model Dog on time helped ease the pain of the night before. Dodging nips from a scrappy Scottish terrier named Haggis kept her very much in the present. The second her mind wandered to Tuni, he sensed it and seized her sleeve and shook it like a dead rodent.

"You just stop that, mister," she said, after the third attack. "I haven't had to muzzle a dog yet. Don't be the first."

"Talking to me?" Carole called from the front counter.

"Haggis," she called back. "He's a biter. Like Fergus the Cairn terrier. I have to stay on my toes."

"I'll put it in their files," Carole said.

"It's okay. I won't forget."

"Where's Tuni today?"

The question was unavoidable, and at least there was a wall between them as she answered. She turned on the water to mask the quaver in her voice. "Gone to Milverton for a month or so."

"What? Why?" Carole appeared in the doorway.

"Cori calls it bootcamp, and I call it finishing school. The upshot is that I want her to be perfectly trained so that I can take her anywhere with me. Like Remi's Leo. Inboard training is faster."

"You poor thing," Carole said. "Does this have anything to do with that dog cop? Rod Crump?"

"No," Sasha said. "Well, maybe. I feel like I'm under scrutiny, and I can't afford the slightest slip up." She looked up from the squirming Scottie. "I'm pretty desperate for this place to succeed, Carole. I won't lie. I've invested everything."

"It'll be fine. You'll see."

Brushing wet hair from her forehead with the back of her free hand, she said, "Hey, no walker!"

"Oh." Carole's hands groped around as if surprised to find she'd left the front desk without it. Holding the wall, she tottered off. "I'm doing better," she called back.

"Great! I'll have you working on dogs in no time."

As she blow-dried the Scottie, her phone danced across the counter. Another text from Griffin. She hadn't read any of them, after the first. His aunt had taken ill, he said. By the time she was settled, it had been too late to join her on the mission. He'd missed work on the gala rehearsal, too.

That may well have been true about his aunt, but there was no reason he couldn't have sent a quick text. He would have, had this mattered to him at all. She wasn't terribly surprised. It only confirmed her first impressions had been correct.

But the texts and phone calls were getting annoying, so she hooked up Haggis' leash and slipped his head through the grooming noose to lock him down. Then she reached for the phone and typed, "No problem. So glad to hear your aunt is doing better." Hopefully that was enough to indicate that she cared about his aunt, but couldn't care less about him. It was true. She was fine on her own, and it was better this way. Apparently, his heart had also been broken before and was beyond repair, just like hers. It had soured him on this town and he'd made it clear he was leaving on the first ship out. Well, smooth sailing to him.

The phone rang and she ignored it. Even restrained, Haggis was a handful, hopping and shifting as she ran the clippers over him. He required her full attention and she wasn't going to listen to Griffin making excuses.

Carol pushed the walker into the doorway and called her name loud enough to be heard over the clippers. "Someone's called the front desk. The name's Deli, I think. She says it's about Tuni and she sounds upset."

"Watch Haggis," she said. "Don't let him move, okay?"

Leaving Carole in the grooming room, she ran to the front desk. Devina the Doggie Doula was barely able to speak at the other end of the phone. She was sobbing. "I just turned my back for a second," she said.

"What happened? Devi, tell me what happened."

"She scaled a seven-foot fence like a monkey. A monkey in a blue dress. She flew off the other side like superman and was gone before I could pry the gate open. But we'll find her, Sasha, I promise. A dog in a dress like that is going to be noticed. I have the entire rescue network on high alert. You just stay where you are for at least two hours, okay? My guess is that she'll be back in one."

"It's snowing, Devi. Her tracks will disappear and she doesn't know your area at all. And she's—"

"I know all that. She's our highest priority right now. Everyone's deploying from Milverton right up to Dorset

Hills. We'll have her back before you know it. Just stay calm."

Impossible. The canine love of her life was on the run in a strange neighborhood.

Calm was no longer in her programming.

"IS SHE AN IDIOT?" Cori said, pacing back and forth across the salon's small sitting area. "You don't take your eyes off a new dog for a single second."

"There was a dog in labor inside and another dog chasing a cat outside. She had her hands full," Bridget said. "Calm down."

"I can't," Cori said. "I recommended Devina for this job, so this is on me."

"It's not on you," Sasha said. "I don't blame anyone. Tuni is like a circus dog."

"Even pregnant," Remi said. "I hope she didn't hurt herself or the pups when she landed."

"Quiet," Cori said.

"No one's here but us," Remi said. "Sash sent Carole home in a cab when she closed the salon."

"Walls have ears." Cori looked angry enough to punch one. Her black gloves had fisted and the orange neon flares were invisible for once. Somehow that made Sasha feel worse than anything. Cori never felt helpless. If she did now, the situation must be dire.

"Devi says the entire rescue network knows about Tuni," she said. "I think the secret's out now."

"The rescue network is confidential," Bridget said. "No one will say a word. As long as we can recover her quickly, it will all die down."

"I want to drive there now," Sasha said. "Why do we have to wait?"

"Just stay cool," Bridget said. "Dogs normally don't go far in these situations. But if they're startled they can bolt and go feral. There's a protocol for recovering lost dogs and it's best to leave it in the hands of experts—and people who know the area well."

"In other words, they can work better and faster without people getting emotional," Cori said.

"People meaning me," Sasha said.

"And her," Cori pointed at Remi. "The rest of us stay cool. Detached. Clinical."

If that were true, her orange neon flares would be visible. But there was no point arguing.

"We'll drive down in an hour," Bridget said. "We need to gather the troops."

The troops didn't wait. The salon got more and more crowded. In addition to the Mafia, Mim Gardiner showed up with her son, Kyle, and her beautiful blonde best friend, Arianna Torrance. The latter was barely in the door before another woman ambushed her in a bear hug. It was Flynn Strathmore, the cartoonist, along with her husband, Denver. With every person that crammed through the door of the little shop, Cori got more subdued. Finally she jumped onto the pew and clapped her hands. Even with the gloves, it made enough noise to silence everyone.

"Okay people, I can't stand another moment jammed in here with you. We are going to deploy. Divide up in as few cars as you can. I want you on speaker in every car, because I am going to explain exactly how you recover a lost dog in winter. There's a protocol for a reason, and one wrong move could send this girl farther afield. Got it?"

"Got it," a dozen voices called out.

Sasha's eyes blurred with tears again, marvelling over the support she had in this community. She wished she didn't have to find out the hard way, but it was still a small miracle.

The door rang again and somehow two more bodies forced their way in. One belonged to a tall man with blazing green eyes under a reindeer toque. Griffin Granger.

Sasha's eyes bounced right off him to the other man, who eased carefully into an open space in a corner. She pushed through the crowd toward him. "Oh Bart, she's gone. My baby's gone."

He shook his head. "Don't let your imagination run all over, now. Tuni is many things but she's not stupid. My guess is that phone is going to ring any second now if you don't fly out of here half-cocked."

"But she's—"

He grabbed her cheek and gave it a none-too-gentle pinch. "Five-four-three-two—"

Six phones rang at once, including Sasha's cell, the business line and Cori's among others. Six phones rose to ears. Six voices shouted: "FOUND."

"She's fine," Cori said, still listening. "Wait... this is apparently important: the dress is unscathed."

Everyone laughed and it broke the tension. Bart opened his jacket and produced a bottle of sparkling wine.

"You were so sure?" Sasha asked. Sometimes it seemed like he tapped into a network even deeper and wider than the Mafia's.

His eyes twinkled. "I just get a feeling sometimes. Now toast to your girl, and talk to that young man. I don't want to hear another word out of him. He thinks I'll help him make his case, but this is as far as I'll go. A young man needs to fight for what he wants in this world."

Sasha moved to hug him but as usual, he pulled away. "Old bones. We crush easily at this age."

He handed the bottle of wine to Remi, and by the time the cork was pulled, Bart had disappeared. Vanished. Ghosted. But unlike most people, he always came back.

CHAPTER TWENTY-FIVE

Flipping the sign to "open" the next morning, Sasha tried to keep her eyes up and straight ahead. They kept wanting to drift down in search of her best buddy. And when they didn't find her, they kept filling with tears. This had been going on pretty much constantly, and she wondered if it would ever stop. If not, her eyelids would never recover from the constant chafing. There was a trail of tissues behind her.

Carole had asked to come in and work an extra shift but Sasha wanted to be alone. It wasn't like she needed help, having rescheduled her clients for the day. Instead, she'd catch up on paperwork and give the place a good clean. Solo busywork was exactly what she needed to recuperate.

The bells rang and Griffin stood in the doorway, waiting for her okay to enter. "It says 'open,'" he said.

"My mistake." She crossed to flip the sign. "I'm really not open for business at all. Sorry."

"Look, I know you're upset, but you've got to hear me out."

"I don't have to do anything. It's my shop. I get to close it when I feel like it."

"Fine then," he said. "I'll have to bring in my secret weapon."

The second he left the salon, she tried to lock the door, but he had managed to duct tape the lock. Before she could peel it off, Grover was pushing into the store. His whole chunky body wriggled and he pushed her backwards across the seating area against the counter. He had her pinned, with his head between her shins.

"Oh Grover, allow me some dignity," she said. "I've had a rough couple of days."

Griffin walked over and pulled Grover out by his hind legs, like a wheelbarrow. "I'm really sorry about Saturday," he said. "My aunt fainted and they rushed her into surgery. It looked touch and go, it really did, but she ended up only needing a pacemaker. She's fine now. But I couldn't use my phone for part of the time and the other part I was fielding calls from a hundred relatives. I called you the minute she was stable."

"I'm so glad she's okay. There's no need to explain. Really."

"There is. Really. Because now you're thinking I'm the kind of guy you can't depend on and my aunt would tell you otherwise. I just couldn't be in two places at once that day."

"Why are you bothering with all of this? You don't even know for sure Tuni's pups are Grover's."

"I know they are."

Her eyes shot up to meet his. "*Know* they are?"

"Well, I don't know it as in I saw anything. It just seems like the most likely scenario given the circumstances."

"I guess time will tell."

"What I'm really trying to say..." He stopped and knelt beside Grover. "Is that I *hope* they are."

A laugh escaped in spite of herself. "Now you *want* these little oddball pups?"

"I'm keeping one, for sure. I bet my family takes all of them, actually. Only the best owners for Grover's pups."

"Well, I have people, too. There's only six, the vet says."

"We can fight over them later," he said, standing again. "What I also wanted to say is that I hope we can do this together. If we can dodge all the politics, it will be fun. We can drive down every night and see the pups. We need to make sure they're socialized properly. There's a short window."

"You've been doing your research, obviously."

His smile was sheepish. "A little. I remember it all went too fast. We had a litter of puppies when I was a kid, remember?"

"Right. Like Christmas, you said."

He nodded. "Christmas for real. Not fake Christmas, like Dorset Hills does it."

"I thought it was lovely here at Christmas. We have different taste, as you've pointed out many times." She gestured to the rack of dog gowns against the wall. "I love doggie couture, for starters. I would put all the puppies in pretty frocks."

"I get some say in this, right?"

"You don't actually. Unless a puppy blood test proves paternity."

His eyebrows soared. "You think it won't be obvious the second they pop out? Grover's distinctive."

The dog's broad wrinkled face tipped up and his droopy eyes stared. It was very hard to imagine his genes wouldn't be readily apparent.

"Well, they would certainly have a great temperament," she said. Looking over Griffin's shoulder, she said, "Uh-oh. Run to the grooming room and take Grover. *Now*. Hide till I tell you to come out."

"I'm not running anywhere. Hide from what?"

"The dog cop! He's just getting out of his car and I'm guessing I'm his lucky target. The last thing either of us needs is trouble with the CCD."

Griffin hauled on Grover's lead while she pushed from the other end, and they got the big dog rolling in the right direction. When she turned back, Rod Crump had stepped onto the sidewalk. Today was the day his luck ran out, and when he hit the patch of ice that typically defeated everyone but him, he started to go down. His arms spun wildly and he clipped an elderly woman in the head. She turned and whacked him with her purse and that sent him down to his knees. He needed to grab the lamppost to get back up.

If Sasha hadn't been so scared, she'd have laughed. At least it gave her hope that the visit wasn't an automatic win for Officer Crump.

"Good morning," she said, when he finally pushed open the door. "How are you feeling after your trip?"

"Funny." He brushed the snow off his pants. "Glad you're in such good spirits." He handed her a dirty, wet envelope. "This won't come as such a shock, then."

Her hands trembled as she pried open the limp flap. The CCD letterhead was dirty and stained. Under it the print was running together, but it was still legible.

"I've been summoned to dog court? What for?"

"Keep reading."

She scanned the page but the legalese blurred before her eyes. "I don't understand."

"Let me make it easy for you," he said. "You'll be aware of the new neuter bylaw, of course. And as I understand it, your dog is not only not spayed, but pregnant."

"You have no evidence of that. She's not even here."

"I have all the evidence I need. And it will come out in court before the pups are even born. Your hearing is tomorrow afternoon."

"Tomorrow! This is a complete ambush."

He shrugged. "I suggest you collect Petunia from wherever you've stashed her. She's expected to be expecting in the courtroom." He laughed at his own wordplay.

"What happens if I don't?"

"Don't what?"

"Show up in court."

"The City will take appropriate action. I would expect The Model Dog would leave the runway. If not worse."

She held open the door. "I think you should go. I'll be checking with my legal advisors."

He crossed in front of her. "Good luck with that."

Closing the door, she leaned against it, breathing heavily. Every day it was a new hit, it seemed. She didn't know how much more she could take without screaming.

Behind her the door jiggled. "Just. Go. AWAY."

"Sasha? I just want to talk."

The voice was barely audible. Definitely not Officer Crump's. Definitely familiar.

She turned and faced her fiancé.

EX-FIANCÉ, she reminded herself as she opened the door.

"Lawrence, what are you doing here?" she said as he eased past her. "What do you want?"

"To see how you're doing. I heard you might be... I don't know... struggling?"

"Heard from whom?"

"Does it matter? Are you? Struggling, I mean. You look like you've been crying. How's Tuni?" He looked around. "*Where's* Tuni?"

"She's away. Visiting friends."

Lawrence was shorter than she remembered. He'd always seemed like a large presence but he was only five foot eight, she figured. His hair had had silvery strands from the time he was 25 and that gave him a more distinguished air than he really deserved.

"Friends?" he said. "Does she do sleepovers and things? Like a regular teenager?"

She knew he was just trying to be light, but her hackles rose anyway. "Why do you care? You abandoned her."

"I did not abandon her." His brow furrowed over deep-set dark eyes. She'd found them smoldering once; now they looked cold. "You wanted to keep her, remember?"

She remembered not wanting him to go. She remembered not wanting him to stay. She remembered clinging to Tuni like a life raft on a stormy sea. And now look what had happened. She'd taken them both down.

"Lawrence, you left us. You left *me* in terrible shape."

He backed toward the door, and she didn't stand in his way. "You were fine. You said you were fine."

"Physically, I was fine. Mentally I was... the opposite of fine."

"But you didn't want a baby. You said you didn't want kids. I thought you were glad it didn't... happen."

She stared at him, first in shock and then revulsion. How had she ever loved him enough to think she could spend the rest of her life with him? What had she been thinking?

"Lawrence, you still don't understand. I don't think you can, actually. So, could you please just go?"

"At least let me pay Tuni's vet bills."

"You want to pay her bills *now*?"

"All the first-year bills mount up. I got my own dog, you know. Not a Welshie this time. They're too crazy. I got a nice, calm pug. Suits my lifestyle better."

"I don't need your money. As you can see—" she gestured around the salon "—I'm managing just fine."

"You're not fine. That's your problem, Sash. Telling people you're fine when you're not. How's anyone supposed to figure out how to help, or where they even fit?"

She glared at him. "The engagement ring you gave me fit. That was your first clue. I'll send that back to you soon, by the way."

"Why don't we meet for—"

She opened the door again. "Goodbye, Lawrence. I wish you the best with your pug."

THERE WAS a sound from the back, and she suddenly remembered that Griffin was still there. He'd probably heard everything. Now he knew she'd been deserted after a terrible miscarriage by a guy who didn't even realize it would rock her world. By a guy who thought she'd be *glad* about losing a baby. By a guy who didn't know her at all, yet had pledged to be her husband.

It was the last straw. In that moment, all she could do was open the door, walk out of her own salon and run down the street.

She hit the same ice patch Officer Crump had. Unlike him, by some miracle, she skated over it and kept right on running.

CHAPTER TWENTY-SIX

The door was still unlocked when she came back that evening. It was dark inside and she screamed when she turned on the lights and saw a prostrate body on the pew.

Griffin sat up and rubbed his eyes. "Ouch. You're hurting our ears."

Under the pew, Grover stirred but couldn't be bothered to get up.

"What are you doing here?" she asked.

"Well, I couldn't leave your shop unlocked," he said. "Someone could have stolen all the frocks. And then what would our puppies wear?"

She tried to smile and failed. "Thank you for guarding the shop. You can go. I'll close up now."

"How was she?"

"Who?"

"Tuni. I figured you'd drive down and see your dog." He checked his phone. "Just enough time to get there and back with an hour of fun with your girl."

This time she did smile. "I did go to see her but I just sat outside. I didn't want to upset her again." Instead, she'd sat in the car crying, while Mim Gardiner talked some sense into her long distance.

Tapping his fingers nervously on the pew, he said, "No offence, Sasha, but your ex sounds like a jerk."

"Hence the 'ex' part."

"He really left you right after a...?" His voice trailed off, as if he couldn't say the word.

"A miscarriage. Yes. We hadn't planned on kids, so it came as a surprise. Lawrence wasn't happy, so I guess he assumed I'd be unhappy, too. But I wasn't unhappy at all about the baby, although I wasn't happy with him. Then I ran into complications and ended up in the hospital for a week."

"You okay now?" He used his sleeve to rub a mark on the pew, and she saw he'd spent hours polishing it while she was gone. The old wood gleamed now.

She nodded. "Seems so. My chances of another pregnancy are lower."

"I'm sorry. You'd make a great mom, you know. I can tell."

Tears welled in her eyes. "That's kind of you to say, but unfortunately just not true. Everything I touch turns to crap." She reached up and took the stuffed spaniel off the shelf. "They fired me from the Valentine's gala planning committee today."

"Why? They were lucky to have you." He pulled a rag out of his coat pocket and started buffing again feverishly.

"The City heard about my day in dog court and decided I'm not gala material. And the people I got to donate to the prize withdrew their support. So now there's no incentive for people to participate."

"Look on the bright side," he said, getting up and

coming over. "Things couldn't get any worse."

She pressed her index finger to her lips. "Don't even say that. It's tempting fate. It could most certainly get worse and I have a lot to be grateful for."

He grabbed her hand and held it. Then he kissed her fingers. "You're not alone."

"I know. That I do know." She stared at him, suddenly struggling for breath as her heart did strange things to her chest. Griffin had always seemed bigger and more masculine than Lawrence, but now it was like they were different breeds altogether. Her hand looked small and fragile in his, not like her own at all. And when his fingers twined through hers, she didn't pull away. *Couldn't* pull away. It was good to have something to hold onto, at least for a moment.

"It's going to be okay," he said, squeezing her hand. "But how did the City find out about Tuni?"

She reclaimed her hand and sat down, turning the stuffed dog over and over. "I don't know. The rescue network must not be as reliable as Cori says."

Griffin sighed. "I told you the walls have ears."

"Cori always says that, too."

She tossed the stuffed dog up and it fell to the floor with a clunking sound. "That's odd," she said, picking it up. Flipping it, she angled it to the light and then squeezed. "There's something inside that wasn't here before." Under the dog's tail were several neat stitches. They were just like the ones on the doggie dresses, where Carole had removed the manufacturing tags so the dogs didn't shred them and eat them. "Let's cut it open."

Griffin pulled out a penknife and split the stitches. She poked around inside until she found a plastic and metal object and pulled it out.

"That's a nanny cam," he said. Turning the stuffed dog, he showed her where the lens had poked through. "Who'd do something like that?"

"I know exactly where we can find out."

CAROLE REVEALED a hairstylist's secret when she opened the door: a purple satin scarf wrapped around her gray curls. It kept the frizz at bay. Sasha sometimes used one herself.

"What's wrong, dear?" she said. "You look like you've been through hell and back."

Sasha gave her a wan smile. "Not back yet, I'm afraid. Do you mind if we come in for a few minutes? I'm sorry it's so late."

Stepping back, Carole let them pass. "It's fine. Just watch out for Caesar. He really doesn't like men."

The living room looked like a bomb had gone off in a flower shop. There were floral prints on the furniture, the curtains, and even the carpet. Several vases of fake flowers dotted end tables. The only other decorative touch was several large paintings of dogs past and present.

Sasha sat on the couch and Griffin hovered uneasily until she pulled him down. "This is Griffin Granger, Carole. Have you met?"

"No, but I've seen you and Grover around. He's a lovely dog." She sat in a big armchair and lifted Caesar into her lap. His lip lifted whenever Griffin moved. "How's Tuni? Has she settled down after her escape?"

"She's well, yes. You know she's expecting puppies, I assume."

Carole's face froze. Then her mouth worked but

nothing came out.

"I know you've heard, Carole. It's all over town, now. And no one is better connected than you."

"Well. That's very kind of you to say, Sasha. I assumed you're very upset about it."

"Not about that, no." Sasha grabbed Griffin's hand between the sofa cushions and squeezed it. Having him here gave her courage, or at least bravado. "I'm looking forward to meeting my furry grandchildren sometime soon."

"Really. Well." Carole batted her eyelids a few times. "That's good, I guess."

"Not everyone agrees, of course. I'm due in dog court tomorrow afternoon. Officer Crump is making a big deal out of the fact that Tuni is..."

"Knocked up?" Griffin said.

"Yes, exactly. By Grover, we assume."

"Oh no!" Carole said. "That would be awful." She covered her mouth. "I'm sorry, Griffin, but it would. They'd be an ab— Never mind."

"Abomination?" he asked, helpfully.

"That's not what I was going to say." She straightened her shoulders. "I'm sure Tuni's puppies will be adorable."

"I really just wanted to ask if you knew how Officer Crump found out about Tuni. Only a very few knew before today."

"I wasn't one of them," Carole said.

Sasha reached into her bag. "Bart's little spaniel was. Turns out he was keeping an eye on the place. The camera was stitched in nicely."

Caesar stood on Carole's knees and started a rolling growl. "That proves nothing," she said.

"No, but the footage of you adjusting it constantly is certainly suggestive. I think you forgot about it sometimes. I couldn't believe you came over every single day to water the sidewalk. Someone could have cracked their head open. But I did love the moment where you went across to Crackers after closing and sprayed their sign with graffiti."

Carole pressed her lips together. Her hand dropped on Caesar; he turned and air snapped.

"Lotus Fiore's a bit of a nutjob," Griffin said. "She went off on Grover once, and all he did was lift his leg on the lamppost."

Carole's eyes were suddenly entreating. "Lotus complained to the city about Caesar. She said he nipped her."

"I'd nip her if I were Caesar," Griffin said. "Did he break the skin?"

"Not at all. Barely a mark on her. She's lobbing complaints at the CCD right left and center and she has their ear, it seems."

"So Officer Crump came to you to discuss Caesar."

She nodded. "He threatened to take me to court. I was afraid of losing Caesar. They sent away Guido, and Frank Bertucci pretty much had a breakdown. All because of Lotus Fiore. Now she has a bead on Caesar."

"And you had to offer him something in return for letting Caesar off the hook?"

"Not Tuni, if that's what you're thinking. I would never agree to hurt a dog."

Now, Sasha was surprised. "Well, what then? What else would make him back off Caesar?"

"I really can't say." Carole pressed her lips together again.

"Is it about me? About something I did at the salon?"

Lips still sealed, Carole shook her head.

"Look Carole, I go to court tomorrow. I can go over

every second of this footage until I figure it out or you can just tell me. I don't think you really want to hurt me or Tuni. But if you don't tell me what they're really after, they might take Tuni away from me. And who knows what they'd do with her pups? You're a dog lover, of that I have no doubt. Do you want these babies on your conscience?"

Her fingers dug into the floral upholstery and then she blurted, "They want the little one."

"The little one?"

"The vicious little one with the Audrey Hepburn cut and the orange fingers. You did a nice job on her hair, by the way. I came by the day you toured my place and saw you cutting."

"Carole, do you even need that walker, or is it a prop?"

She threw herself back into the embrace of daisy petals and groaned. "Oh, this whole thing got out of control. Yes, I injured my leg, but it wasn't that bad. The City drove me out because of Caesar."

"They wrecked your business for one nip?"

"It wasn't just one. But yes, that's what we've come to in Dorset Hills. One or two wrong moves by a dog and your lease is simply up. You're out of business and a dog groomer fresh out of school takes over." She pulled off her purple scarf and churned her fingers through her hair. "They told me if I gave them what they needed on the little one they'd let me have my shop back."

"And run me out of it?"

"You can get work anywhere. You're young and talented and pretty."

"With a reputation in tatters, partly thanks to you."

"I can't help what they did with the information. I agreed to work for you, and manage the camera, that's all. I'll deny it, of course."

Sasha signaled to Griffin. "Let's go. I've heard enough to know I'm going down in court tomorrow."

"You won't be the first, and you won't be the last," Carole said. "You'll be fine."

"Thanks for your support, Carole. Your granddaughter must be proud."

"Don't bother trying to shame me," Carole said, hurrying ahead with no trace of a limp. "It's every man for himself in this town now. Like a wildlife survival show."

"I'll come armed to court tomorrow."

"I'll be there to see it," she said. "And the sooner you can get your things out of my salon, the better."

Caesar grabbed Griffin's pant cuff and he tried to shake him off. The dog didn't let go. "This dog's not neutered, is he? So hard to tell with these small dudes."

"He didn't need to be," Carole said. "His testicles never descended."

"Ouch. Sounds uncomfortable." Griffin winced and managed to push the dog away with his other foot. "No wonder he bites everyone."

"I guess the City is going to fire you when they hear about Grover running around knocking up the ladies. I feel bad for your Aunt Helen. She'll never get back what you owe her now."

Griffin took a step forward and Caesar simultaneously lunged. The dog caught his jeans about midthigh and just hung there. Sasha snapped a quick photo with her phone as Carole disengaged the dog.

"That's just a little too close for comfort, no?" Sasha said, as they left.

"I underestimated him," Griffin said, sheepishly. "Turns out he really was hiding a pair."

CHAPTER TWENTY-SEVEN

Sasha arrived for her day in court in Bridget's lime-green van. It was a miracle they made it alive, because Cori was driving, and her neon orange flipping fingers seemed to be anywhere but on the wheel.

"Are you really that surprised you're the CCD's main target?" Bridget asked, from the passenger seat. "You're the head of the Rescue Mafia."

"I thought you were," Cori said, grinning at her.

"No, I'm the voice of reason. Most of the time."

"And I'm the voice of reason the rest of the time," Duff said, from Sasha's left.

"I just take orders," Nika said, from Sasha's right.

"Me, too," Maisie said, also from Sasha's right.

It should have felt crowded, but instead it felt cozy—as if they were going on an all-girl adventure, instead of a potentially career-ending mission. She looked around at the faces, all of them animated, and was amazed at how much her life had changed in two short months. Then she was lonely and lost; now she had a pack. Perhaps it had come at a price, but it was still more valuable than she could have imagined.

Remi had tried to come, too, but there was no room in the van. So she drove with Mim Gardiner, Ari Torrance and Flynn Strathmore. It was going to be a full house. She hoped the show was worth everyone taking time off work.

"I wish I could represent you, like I did with other defendants last month," Cori said. "But I got banned from the courtroom when Marti Forrester left."

"I thought the mayor would give this up," Duff said. "It doesn't look good politically. The story is getting out about the City treating dogs unfairly. That's going to affect the Dog Town brand."

"Off the record, Mike said the mayor wanted to back away from dog court. But Cliff Whorley has promised he can turn this around. He's got a month to do it, apparently."

"Great, so I'm the poster girl for Cliff's crusade," Sasha said. "How will he gain points by throwing a groomer and her pregnant dog under the bus?"

"Remember, the Rescue Mafia is the real target," Bridget said. "He wants to use you to get to us."

"Well, I'm not playing his game."

"It could get dirty," Cori said. "He could threaten to seize Tuni and her pups."

"He wouldn't."

Cori and Bridget exchanged glances. "He might."

"If he did, you could get her back, right?"

Bridget craned around to meet Sasha's eyes. "We would most certainly do our best, and we've succeeded before. But there's always a chance they could outsmart us."

"Unlikely," Cori said. "That's why they want to take me down."

"What happened with Kinney Butterfield?" Nika

asked. "I thought she was going to find out what the CCD was planning."

"Useless," Cori said. "It's been a week and nothing. Good thing we didn't hand over the puppy mill info yet."

"Don't count her out," Bridget said. "She's just under extreme scrutiny. Cliff Whorley thinks she helped Marti expose flaws in the CCD, so she has to tread lightly or be in his sights, too. She can't help us if she's fired."

Sasha groaned. "How deep does this mess go?"

"We're stuck in the biggest pile of crap ever," Cori said.

"All you can do is keep your chin up as high as you can," Duff said. "And know we are here for you."

The women crowded in closer to Sasha on either side, till she could barely breathe. It was the next best thing to a group hug, and she was grateful for it.

"Just stay cool," Cori said. "Remember what I told you. You get flustered, you lose."

A bead of sweat rolled down her forehead. "Cool is my middle name. I'll make you proud."

"No nooses today," Duff said. "But use everything else you've got."

THE COURTROOM WAS CHILLY, which helped initially with staying cool, but it would eventually start having the reverse effect. She figured that was part of their strategy: keep the defendants shivering and fearing for survival. Kinney Butterfield showed her to her place in the first row. "Good luck," she whispered, shaking Sasha's hand. When she pulled away, a little slip of paper stayed in Sasha's palm. She slipped it into her pocket without looking.

Every seat behind her was taken, and she didn't know whether to be pleased or ashamed. It seemed a long shot that one groomer—a relative newcomer—would be such a big draw. The CCD was making a meal out of something that shouldn't even be an appetizer.

Cliff Whorley swept into the courtroom wearing his judicial robes at two p.m. sharp. His face was florid under a bristling salt and pepper mustache.

"Greetings, Ms. Wildwood," he said, looking down from the dais. "Let's get straight to the point, shall we? My understanding from Officer Rodney Crump is that your dog, Petunia, is not only unspayed, but also pregnant. As you are no doubt aware, Dorset Hills' new bylaw states that all dogs must be spayed by age eight months unless the owner has a breeder's license or a valid reason, verified by a veterinarian."

"Yes, sir," Sasha said. "I have a statement from not one but two veterinarians confirming that they refused to spay Tuni in advance of her first birthday. She had a serious infection that made the surgery risky."

She passed the veterinary statements along the row to Kinney Butterfield, who was standing at the end. During the commotion, she managed a peek at the note Kinney had given her.

"And yet you saw fit to breed Petunia," Cliff continued. "Despite these health conditions? How did the vets feel about that?"

Sasha glanced over her shoulder at Griffin and he gave her a quick nod of encouragement. Bartholomew Barnes sat beside him, hands crossed over the top of his cane. He raised one finger toward Cliff in a subtle salute: his middle one.

She turned back to the judge, squared her shoulders

and continued. "I would never have chosen to breed Tuni, judge. She made that decision for herself, I'm afraid. I was taking a grooming course to better myself as a citizen of this town, and my caregiver didn't notice she had escaped."

"In fact, you hadn't noticed your dog was in heat, as I understand it. And therefore had not warned your caregiver to take extra precautions."

Sasha hung her head. "That's true, sir. I've never owned a dog before. That said, the vet noted that a heat may be silent, particularly the first." She passed another statement down the row. "She was seen that week by a vet and there were no signs of estrus then."

"Nevertheless, the onus is on the owner to ensure her dog remains..."

"Pure?" she asked. "Unadulterated? Chaste?"

He glared at her. "'Not pregnant' will do. There's no need to ascribe human virtues to our dogs. They're animals and we're responsible for them. Knowing that Tuni might come into heat at any time, it was your duty to keep her—"

"A virgin. I know. Trust me, I was pretty upset when I found out about her loss of innocence."

"Ms. Wildwood. Stick to the point, please. The point is that she dug her way out of the yard, was missing for half an hour, and came home pregnant. You didn't notice for some time."

"I didn't notice at all. Until someone more knowledgeable about the birds and the bees told me."

"You elected not to spay at that time. Many would."

"I elected to listen to my vet, who cautioned against pregnant spays. I judge no one else for their decisions."

"We have no capacity for unwanted puppies in Dorset Hills, Ms. Wildwood. That's why there's a neuter policy in effect."

"It wasn't in effect when she got pregnant sir, according to my sources. She got pregnant on December 15th and your policy came into effect last week."

"It doesn't work that way."

"It's a clear and valid exception, sir." She pulled in a deep breath and then took her first shot. "Unlike what happened with your son-in-law."

Cliff's already red face turned maroon. "Excuse me? There are no—"

"Unwed mothers in your family? Perhaps not, but if I understand correctly, your daughter's live-in boyfriend's mastiff was castrated just a few days ago. *After* the neuter policy came into effect. Sir, this reeks of hypocrisy."

Rustling papers couldn't disguise Cliff's hoarse breathing as he dealt with the stench. "There's a difference between neutering males and unwanted puppies. I have it on good authority that Petunia's pups were sired by an English bulldog. That sounds like a very risky proposition for your Brittany spaniel."

"She's a Welsh springer, sir. But thank you for your concern. I share it myself. She's had the very best prenatal care, including an ultrasound to prove all is well."

"We'll make sure she gets even better care than you can provide when we take her into custody."

Now Sasha's face flushed. "Why would you seize my dog, sir? Was your grand-dog seized? *My* dog didn't break a law that didn't yet exist."

He waved a dismissive hand. There were three chunky rings on it—enough to make lift off a challenge. "We don't feel Petunia has adequate care. You left her twice with care-givers who allowed her to escape. The poor girl was seen running around Milverton wearing only a dress during a snow storm."

"I had to take her to a home for wayward mothers because of the City's disapproval, sir. After your officer started harassing me at my salon, it seemed safest to move Tuni so she wouldn't be traumatized. We do the best we can for our kids, don't we? I'm sure you wanted more for your daughter, too."

His mustache twitched before he answered. "Petunia will be very well supervised and the pups attended to properly in the CCD's care."

"I refuse to surrender her, sir. I will close my shop and leave Dorset Hills immediately with my dog." She clenched her hands, readying for the next shot. "You can give the space back to Carole's Curls. She said you promised her that in exchange for information on me."

There was a murmur in the crowd and Cliff rapped the gavel smartly. "I did nothing of the kind. And I'll thank you for not bringing slander and red herrings into my courtroom."

"Sir, I—"

Bang, went the gavel. "Silence."

Sasha raised both hands, palms up. "No. I will *not* be silenced. People need to know what's been going on in Dorset Hills. You have spies planting cameras in private establishments to gather evidence to use against us. Unless I'm much mistaken, that's as illegal in Dog Town as it is anywhere else."

"That's a lie." Cliff looked both outraged and confused. "We are not planting cameras anywhere."

"I have witnesses."

He shook his head. "Impossible. No one will testify to that, I'm quite sure of it."

Sasha throat almost seized. She hadn't taped Carole's confession, and no doubt they'd find a way to twist this inside out. But she didn't have the luxury of giving up now because Tuni depended on her. "What you're doing here is ridiculous. Bringing people in on a day's notice, and turning neighbor against neighbor. It's not what this community is all about."

Bang. Bang.

The gavel wasn't enough to silence the crowd, so several dog officers moved into the rows, urging people to sit. When Kinney reached Sasha, she winked. It was enough to give her strength to continue.

"I'm a newcomer to Dorset Hills," she called out. "I love this town and I love my dog. But if the City is turning against dogs and dog-lovers, I'm taking my dog and going."

"It's too late," Cliff called over the mutterings. "We've already taken your dog."

Now there was an audible gasp, 30 people strong.

Sasha's stomach twisted into a knot. She could only hope from Kinney's wink that it was not the case. If they had, she would get Tuni back, no matter what. At any rate, she was not going down without a fight. A big one. All the fury she'd felt in the past six weeks came to a rolling boil.

"You wouldn't dare seize my dog from another jurisdiction."

"Wouldn't we?"

"You wouldn't, sir. Because it would be stupid. And despite everything that's said about you, and about dog court, no one thinks you're stupid."

There was a titter throughout the courtroom, and Cliff gave a menacing sweep of his gavel instead of banging it. "I'm smart enough to set an example for this city, young lady."

"You're making me a scapegoat but it won't work. Everyone knows the mayor doesn't want more bad press.

But if the planted camera isn't enough, maybe what I've got on my tablet will be. Permission to approach the bench, judge?"

"Declined."

The unfairness of it all drove her forward anyway. "Reconsider, sir. I have evidence that I assume you'll want to see."

"You assume incorrectly."

Halfway to the bench, she stopped. "All right. I guess I'll just add it to the new social media campaign residents are creating to bring fairness back to Dog Town."

He twisted his rings for a moment and then nodded. "Approach."

Sasha's hands shook as she presented her tablet to him. "Scroll through, sir. You'll see some photos I took at recent events around the city. There are more unneutered dogs than you'd expect. Some people have taken to hiding their dogs' privates with custom clothing, but I still got some good shots."

"This is just ... unseemly," Cliff said, his ringed fingers flipping faster and faster.

"They're animals, sir, like you said. But I'm afraid you have your work cut out for you. Some of our founding families have chosen to keep their dogs intact. I hope you'll choose to make an example out of them as you have with Tuni."

Cliff rose and swept off the dais with Sasha's tablet in hand. The slam as he left reverberated through the courtroom. And then the applause started.

CHAPTER TWENTY-EIGHT

Sasha hoisted the train of her long blue dress as she walked up the stairs onto the stage at the Elgin Theater. Tuni couldn't be with her, but at her side was the next best spotted thing: Leo. Remi had gladly offered Leo as Sasha's date. He not only gave her courage, but he was also arguably the most popular dog in town. It seemed highly unlikely that the catcalls were for her, although she did look good. Very good, if Griffin Granger's expression were to be trusted.

Head held high, she swept down the catwalk, turned once, turned twice and then, just to hammer the point home that she would not be taken down by Dorset Hills' politics, she turned a third time. Leo sailed in an effortless circle in his little grey vest and blue cravat, his tail wagging harder each time. Then he pranced back up the walk, touching his nose to outstretched hands.

"Your dog is a rock star," Sasha said, returning his leash to Remi. She had to lean in so her friend could hear over the music.

"You're a rock star. To go out and own that catwalk after all that's happened is beyond impressive. You won!"

"For now." She shook back her hair and smiled. "I wouldn't put it past these guys to find a new loophole but we're okay for now, unless the City wants to take down every high-profile owner of unneutered dogs."

"You were so smart to take all those photos at events."

"It was Bart's doing," she said. "He was always telling me to keep my eyes open and then at the wedding he insisted I take photos. He said it was to bombard his niece but maybe he knew something was afoot with the CCD. If he did, he's admitting to nothing. Typical Bart."

"Well, you're the one who put the pieces together—under pressure."

"I hadn't planned to use the naughty canine crotch shots until Cliff said he'd seized Tuni already. Little did I know that Kinney had tipped Cori off so she could have her moved to a safe house. She'd already given me the dirt on Cliff's grand-dog."

"Thanks to your courage in standing up for what's right, every dog owner can breathe a little easier right now."

"Kinney told Cori the dog cop is dirty. She's going after him before he can get a case together on the Mafia. And for that Cori's feeding her enough information to keep the CCD well distracted. What a mess."

"This will all simmer down," Remi said. "Things go in cycles. Dog Town boomed and now it's at risk of going bust if Council isn't careful. But for tonight, we have a Valentine's king and queen to anoint."

She pointed to twin gilt thrones the set designers had created under Griffin's supervision. He'd said it galled him to participate in such Dog Town foolishness, but for the sake of keeping his job, he did it with a smile. Sasha sensed he actually enjoyed it.

A new tune blared, and the first bachelor started down the runway. The catcalls were louder now, because the audience comprised mostly women. Out of the wings the next bachelor emerged. It was Griffin Granger, resplendent in a black tuxedo. A top hat concealed the frizz of auburn hair that now covered his head. At his side, Grover was wearing a matching outfit, sized down.

Griffin walked with an easy gait to the end of the catwalk and Grover trundled along, raising even more cheers. At the end, Griffin spun on his heel while Grover just stood there, staring around. Then Griffin turned and caught Sasha's eye. He doffed the top hat and gave a deep bow. Then he issued a command to Grover, who did his best to offer a play bow. The crowd went wild.

Sasha fanned herself with her program and curtsied back.

"Man, you two are working it," Remi said. "You must want that prize."

"Who wouldn't?" she said. "It's even more amazing than before."

The wealthy donors had not stepped back up. They were too offended by the City's scrutiny over their dogs' private parts to play along with Valentine's Day. Remi had other strings to pull, however, and pull she did. Hannah Pemberton, of the billionaire Pemberton family, had funded a romantic evening for the happy winners at the Larkson Grand Hotel, and pitched in five thousand dollars for the service dog fundraiser as well. The event was a success no matter what.

"Or maybe you just really want the guy," Remi said. "Now he's your Dog Town dream come true, no?"

"The crowd can decide. But he certainly made an effort tonight... by having the good sense to enlist your help."

"Good thing I still had a key to your shop. I got the tux and took it to a professional for alterations. That dog is a tank."

Remi rushed off and Sasha enjoyed the view from the wings. She would never have had as much fun if she hadn't been kicked off the committee. Bart was right: sometimes things work out far better if you can just let them unfold.

When the votes came in, she was named the Valentine's Bachelorette and Griffin the Bachelor. He had probably tipped the crowd in his favor with the flourishes, but everyone loves a lover. When he bowed again and took her hand, she stepped out happily. Down the runway they went again. This time Grover put on his brakes, and then tipped over on his side and played dead. Griffin threw up his hands in mock despair and the crowd laughed and applauded. Dropping the lead, he led Sasha to the end of the runway. Swishing her train aside, he dipped her backwards and kissed her.

It should have felt staged and awkward—it *was* staged and awkward—but somehow, when his lips touched hers, it also felt sincere, and real and just right. She grabbed his shoulder, and he swung her around in a deep arc so that everyone could see what Dog Town politics could do when used for good.

Her head was spinning as he led her off the stage, and she clung to his arm. Luckily Grover found his paws and left under his own steam.

Remi was waving her arms to get Sasha's attention. "It's time," she called.

"It's time," Sasha said to Griffin.

"Come on, Grandma," he said, squeezing her hand. "Let's see your pups come into the world."

GRIFFIN WAS a little green around the gills by the time the last of six pups emerged four hours later. Devi the Doggie Doula had come into the City to oversee the delivery in Sasha's apartment. The vet had been on standby, but Tuni managed like a pro. One pup after another came off the assembly line and Devi made sure they started feeding.

"Does it really feel like Christmas?" Sasha asked, grinning at Griffin.

"Absolutely," he said. "And Halloween at the same time. I didn't remember it being so... earthy."

"Yeah, I watched some videos to make sure I could support Tuni without fainting."

"Sasha." He peered into the kids' swimming pool Devi had set up to hold the litter. "I'm going to state the obvious here and I hope you won't be upset."

"It's okay. What is it?"

"These pups aren't Grover's. Every last one of them is brown and white. They all look like miniature versions of Tuni."

"They're only a few inches long," she said. "We'll know more when they get some beef on them."

Devi shook her head. "I've seen pups of every persuasion in rescue, and my educated guess is that these are not bulldog crosses."

Griffin's face fell. He really had wanted them to be Grover's.

"It doesn't matter who sires puppies but who raises

them, right?" Sasha said. "So they're still yours. And you'll have first pick of the litter." She reached across the pool and squeezed his hand. "I want to send each one home with one of your beautiful doghouses. Now that you've bought into the cheesy side of Dog Town, your business is going to skyrocket."

"Good," he said, laughing. "Because I'll probably get the boot from my city job unless I get Grover snipped."

"Wait for the City's next move," Sasha said. "They're recalibrating as we speak."

Devi left the room with a pile of dirty towels, and Griffin pulled Sasha across the hardwood floor.

"We're going to make people work for these puppies," he said. "I'm doing background checks on everyone to make sure they're worthy."

"Why not a spy cam?" Sasha said. "I've got one on hand."

"I like the way you think," he said.

"Does this mean you're not shipping out of Dog Town anytime soon?"

"Are you crazy?" He wrapped his arms around her and squeezed. "I can't leave my grandkids. Ever."

Then he kissed her again. It was a lot less glamorous here in her dingy apartment beside a tub full of squealing puppies, but it felt like Christmas all over, and done right this time.

CHAPTER TWENTY-NINE

The bells rang and Bart shuffled into the salon with Puck ambling behind him. "What's so important that we had to come out on a cold March day?" he said.

"Have a seat," she said, patting the pew beside her. "I have something important to say."

He sighed as he eased himself down, and Puck collapsed at his feet.

Sasha stared at Puck and shook her head. "This dog deserves a good trim, Bart."

"Like I always say, no one likes a bossy groomer."

She leaned over and scratched Puck's chest, and he rolled onto his side to expose his belly. "Well, there it is then."

"There what is?"

She looked up at Bart and raised an eyebrow. "It. The begetter of puppies. Now I see why you keep Puck's hair long."

"Never you mind. I've lived here all my life and the City can't tell me what to do with my dog. If a man can control his dog, there's no need to alter him."

"But what if he can't? Control his dog, that is. What if the dog sires a litter at the advanced age of ten?"

He crossed his arms on his cane and stared at her. "If you're trying to tell me something, spit it out, girl. We don't know how much time I have left on the planet."

"The vet did bloodwork on Tuni's puppies. It turns out they're pureblood Welsh springer spaniels. So unless she pulled off a spectacular biological feat, it looks like she met up with a Welshie who took her fancy."

"Is this fairy tale going somewhere today?"

"So the vet asked around about Welsh springer spaniels, and the only one any vet in the Greater Dorset Hills area had heard of was a Mr. Puck Barnes."

"Guesswork," he said. "And now you think this old boy had his way with your Petunia? I've never seen him even glance at her. She irritates him. As, frankly, you do me, young lady."

"Well, I would never say anything without doing my due diligence. So I took a look around your back yard."

"You climbed into my yard?"

"It pays to be nimble in Dog Town. I found a nice hole that looked like Tuni's work, but I couldn't be sure, of course. So I jumped in and that's where I found her missing dog tag. I guess when they got frisky, it fell off. Because to my knowledge, she's never been in your yard before."

Bart shrugged. "I can't account for what goes on in my yard when I'm not there. I didn't see anything untoward at any point. So you are free to jump to your own conclusions."

"Well, I conclude, with my vet's support, that Puck is a daddy." She leaned back. "You can come and see your grandchildren when you like. They're adorable, by the way."

"It sounds tiring. Puck isn't up to it, I'm afraid."

She poked the dog with her foot and he just grunted. "Puck isn't up to much, is he?"

Bart shrugged and the way the light hit his glasses put a twinkle in his eye. "He's old, not dead."

"Ah-ha! You know it's true."

"I know nothing except drama follows wherever you go."

"Oh, you like drama, Bart. Otherwise you wouldn't nudge me in the right direction all the time."

This time his shrug was bigger. "Well, you've got a good heart and I don't want to see it crushed. We lost a nice woman in that judge the mayor chased off, and this town can't afford much more of that foolishness."

"I'm not going anywhere," she said, getting up to grab the plush spaniel. "I want to turn The Model Dog into such a raging success that the City stops scheming against me. Carole's going to have to perm someplace else. Permanently."

"That's the spirit. I knew it was in there, waiting to burst out."

"Like a litter of purebred puppies," she said. "Do you have Puck's papers, by the way?"

He shuddered. "I don't care about those things. Can I go now?"

"Sure, but I see the gang's arriving. Do you want to miss them?"

Groaning, he got to his feet just as the door opened and Cori came in with her arms full of a bedraggled brown thing that would probably turn out to be a terrier after two hours of brushing, and bathing and clipping.

"Well, if it isn't Dog Town's most wanted criminal," Bart said, smirking at Cori as she passed him.

"If it isn't Dog Town's most notorious puppy daddy," Cori shot back. Spinning, she managed to flip an orange knit finger before heading into the grooming room like she owned the place.

"No need to worry about that one," Bart said. "This town will never break her."

"It won't break any of us," Duff said, pulling off her hat. "Did you choose your namesake yet? I hear there's a little Welshie Bartholomew waiting to be christened."

"I was already on my way out," he said, opening the door. "No need to chase me."

"Who gets to look after the puppies while you groom the rescue?" Bridget said.

"Remi's there now, and Griffin takes over at five," Sasha said. "Never has there been a better socialized litter. He even reads to them."

"He'll make a great dad someday," Duff said, smiling.

"Never mind," Sasha said.

"One of us has to reproduce, and you're the most normal."

"Hey," Nika said. "I want babies. Human ones, I mean."

"Me too," Maisie said. "We're normal."

"Luckily there are no laws about rescuers reproducing," Bridget said.

"*Yet*," Cori called. "Who knows what the City has in store for us?"

"Bring it on," Sasha said, looking around at the smiling faces. "Dog Town forever."

A pet-phobic PR person uncovers a crime that could bring Dog Town to its knees. Can a curious cat and loveable dog help Evie solve the mystery and find a whole new pet-centered life? Find out in *Nine Lives in Dog Town.*

Please sign up for my author newsletter at **Sandyrideout.com** to receive the FREE prequel, *Ready or Not in Dog Town*, as well as *A Dog with Two Tales*, the prequel to the Bought-the-Farm series. You'll also get the latest news and far too many pet photos.

Before you move on to the next book, if you would be so kind as to leave a review of this one, that would be great. I appreciate the feedback and support. Reviews stoke the fires of my creativity!

Other Books by Sandy Rideout and Ellen Riggs

Dog Town Series:

- *Ready or Not in Dog Town* (The Beginning)
- *Bitter and Sweet in Dog Town* (Labor Day)
- *A Match Made in Dog Town* (Thanksgiving)
- *Lost and Found in Dog Town* (Christmas)
- *Calm and Bright in Dog Town* (Christmas)
- *Tried and True in Dog Town* (New Year's)
- *Yours and Mine in Dog Town* (Valentine's Day)
- *Nine Lives in Dog Town* (Easter)

- *Great and Small in Dog Town* (Memorial Day)
- *Bold and Blue in Dog Town* (Independence Day)
- *Better or Worse in Dog Town* (Labor Day)

Boxed Sets:

- *Mischief in Dog Town - Books 1-3*
- *Mischief in Dog Town - Books 4-7*
- *Mischief in Dog Town - Books 8-10*

Bought-the-Farm Cozy Mystery Series

- *A Dog with Two Tales (prequel)*
- *Dogcatcher in the Rye*
- *Dark Side of the Moo*
- *A Streak of Bad Cluck*
- *Till the Cat Lady Sings*
- *Alpaca Lies*
- *Twas the Bite Before Christmas*
- *Swine and Punishment*
- *Don't Rock the Goat*
- *Swan with the Wind*

Made in the USA
Las Vegas, NV
08 October 2022